Carol Marinelli

VIRGIN'S STOLEN NIGHTS WITH THE BOSS

HARLEQUIN
PRESENTS

HARLEQUIN® PRESENTS™

Recycling programs
for this product may
not exist in your area.

ISBN-13: 978-1-335-59306-1

Virgin's Stolen Nights with the Boss

Copyright © 2023 by Carol Marinelli

Harlequin Enterprises ULC
22 Adelaide St. West, 41st Floor
Toronto, Ontario M5H 4E3, Canada
www.Harlequin.com

Printed in U.S.A.

"Don't…" Elias took her in his arms because it was the only thing to do, or rather it was impossible not to, and she felt the wrap of his arms around her.

"Capricorn…"

"She's snoring," he said, but Carmen knew enough about animals not to transfer her grief and she pushed him away and stumbled out.

He followed her, and she gave a strangled laugh, then the tears shuddered out as she pressed her face and mouth into his chest. She moaned out a sob and felt as if her knees were buckling, but he held her firm. She cried quietly but so deeply and just huddled in his arms and let herself be held for the first time…

"Don't let me go."

"I'm going to kiss you—once," he told her.

"Please." She nodded, because she simply had to know what his kiss was like.

"Once," he warned. "And we never speak of it again, because I do not mess around with my stable hands…"

"Just this once…" She nodded, because she knew he did not.

Heirs to the Romero Empire

A brand-new sizzling Spanish miniseries from
USA TODAY *bestselling author Carol Marinelli.*

Siblings Sebastián, Alejandro and Carmen Romero
are heirs to a renowned sherry empire in Spain.
To the world, they have it all: charm, status and
wealth. But their parents' stormy marriage has
also left the siblings with a legacy of emotional
wariness, which has meant the empire always
came before love. Now is that all about to change?

Read Alejandro's story in
His Innocent for One Spanish Night

Read Sebastián's story in
Midnight Surrender to the Spaniard

And read Carmen's story in
Virgin's Stolen Nights with the Boss

All available now!

Carol Marinelli recently filled in a form asking for her job title. Thrilled to be able to put down her answer, she put "writer." Then it asked what Carol did for relaxation and she put down the truth— "writing." The third question asked for her hobbies. Well, not wanting to look obsessed, she crossed her fingers and answered "swimming"—but, given that the chlorine in the pool does terrible things to her highlights, I'm sure you can guess the real answer!

Books by Carol Marinelli

Harlequin Presents

Cinderellas of Convenience

The Greek's Cinderella Deal
Forbidden to the Powerful Greek

Heirs to the Romero Empire

His Innocent for One Spanish Night
Midnight Surrender to the Spaniard

Scandalous Sicilian Cinderellas

The Sicilian's Defiant Maid
Innocent Until His Forbidden Touch

Visit the Author Profile page
at Harlequin.com for more titles.

For Rosie,

Thank you for being such a brilliant friend!

Carol xxx

PROLOGUE

'*CARMEN, ESTO NO ha terminado...*'
  Carmen, this isn't over.

The suppressed anger in Sebastián Romero's voice would send a chill down many a spine. But for Carmen her older brother's words provoked only a deep sense of weariness.

The three Romero siblings stood in the newly deserted stables.

Her brothers, on hearing that their sister was moving the horses, had dropped everything, driving in urgent convoy from the luxurious sherry bodega that stood in the heart of Jerez out to the sprawling property that was about to become the centre of a bitter legal dispute.

The brothers wore smart suits and shades, and both were a foot taller than Carmen, who stood in jodhpurs and, even in the mid-spring Spanish sun, a jumper.

'Papá always said that he wanted the hacienda to be left to you,' Sebastián insisted. He wanted her to stay and fight. 'Maria only came back when she knew Papá was dying.'

None of the Romero siblings referred to Maria as Mother or Mamá. The title had been dropped individually rather than collectively—one by one, each had chosen to distance themselves in an effort to protect their minds and hearts.

Alejandro chimed in then. 'If you leave now you are handing it to her on a plate!'

'Please, stop.'

Carmen put up her hand to halt them. Her father's death six months ago was still a raw wound that smarted when touched. It was an agonising cocktail of confusion and regret, and he'd left her with so many unanswered questions...

'It's just for three months! Even before Papá died I said I needed a break.'

'She did say that.' Alejandro nodded, addressing their elder brother.

But as he went to put a protective arm around Carmen she pulled away. She felt his sudden tension as he perhaps registered the fragility of her frame beneath the heavy jumper.

'Carmen...' He closed his eyes as he chose his words carefully. 'By rehoming the horses you've made things easier on her.'

'So I should have left them for her to neglect?' Carmen challenged. 'We all know how little she cared for *us*.'

By most standards the Romero siblings were blessed—all were joint heirs to the famed sherry bodega, and properties and investments far beyond Jerez. And while they shared many features, from their raven-black hair to their passionate natures, they were all very different people—be it by nature or nurture, the fires of their childhood had forged three unique personalities.

Sebastián, ten years older than Carmen, was ruthless. His recent marriage to Anna, and pending adoption of Anna's young daughter Willow, might have softened his soul, but not his stance on business. And, to him, their mother Maria de Luca was nasty business. With José Romero dead, he wanted Maria de Luca annihilated—

right down to the image of her being removed from the label of the famed sherry they produced.

Alejandro, five years apart from both Sebastián and Carmen, was more reasonable. He wanted most of their father's last wishes met, and for Maria to remain the face of the brand, but when it came to the family home he was more than prepared to stand up for what he felt was right. The place belonged to his sister.

The legal might of the Romeros was primed and ready for a fight, because the last will and testament of José Romero was being bitterly contested.

As for Carmen...

At twenty-six, she was the baby of the family. She had always been fiery, and sided with Sebastián's strong stance against Maria, but since her father's passing she'd felt increasingly depleted.

'Carmen,' he warned, 'you need to stay and fight this—not run away.'

'I'm not running away.' Carmen's voice was always a little throaty but this morning it sounded strained and hoarse. 'I just need a break.'

'But why America?' Alejandro asked.

'It's the land of the free,' Carmen responded. She had always liked hearing that at school, and had loved the occasions when she had competed there. 'And I want to be free.'

'But why LA?'

'Maybe I want to be a film star or a model...' She fought a rare blush. 'Maybe I want to dance...'

'Carmen, you hate getting dressed up even for the Romero Ball.'

No one but her brothers would know that.

Her hair, when it was out of its ponytail, was glossy and long, and she dazzled on the red carpet on suitable occasions. Away from the spotlight, though, Carmen lived in jodhpurs, or on particularly hot days a bikini and shorts, but had been trying to be a little more glamorous of late.

'And you *abhor* dancing,' Sebastián added, not noticing the press of her lips as he continued his mini lecture. 'As well as that, you don't take direction…'

Carmen shot her brother a look. 'You have no idea how disciplined riding is.'

'I meant outside of riding.'

'I was joking about being an actress,' Carmen said. 'I'm going to work in a café or a restaurant.'

'But why?' Sebastián gave her a nonplussed look. 'It's not as if you need the money.'

'Perhaps I want to prove that I can make it on my own.'

'Carmen,' he said, glancing at her kitten-soft hands— despite a life spent in the stables, she *always* wore gloves. 'I've never seen you take a cup through to the kitchen, let alone wash it. Anyway, you won't last a morning without a horse.'

'I can barely *remember* a morning without a horse.' Carmen sighed. 'And I've never known a moment when I wasn't a Romero…'

'Meaning?'

Her full name was Carmen Romero de Luca, but in Spain she was Carmen Romero, a brilliant and talented equestrian who had trained and performed with the famous Andalusian dancing horses, as well as competing in dressage at the highest levels.

And she was José Romero's only daughter.

People said she was entitled and spoilt.

And that was all true.

But a deeper truth was that she was lonely and scared and seemed to have the worst luck with relationships.

Carmen had overheard her last boyfriend talking about her, saying how demanding and needy she was. She had covered her mouth to silence her cry of anguish. Her mother had, on more than one occasion, accused her of being the very same. They couldn't both be wrong, could they?

The character assassination hadn't ended there, though. She'd listened to the man she had been planning to lose her virginity to that weekend telling his friend that she always smelt of the stables, and that he practically had to hold his nose to kiss her.

His friend's response: 'Just close your eyes and think of all that Romero money...'

But actually it wasn't her ex who had broken her heart—her mother had inflicted that damage a long time before. And now, at the grand old age of twenty-six, Carmen was starting to believe that it might be safer to carry her broken heart all the way to the grave rather than risk attempting to love again.

She looked at her brothers. They had the same dark eyes as her, the same glossy black hair and olive skin, and they shared the same DNA. Yet even though they came from the same broken home her brothers were so self-assured, so confident...

Carmen only pretended to be.

And, while it was true she was spoilt and precious—she'd been her father's favourite, after all—Carmen would trade it all for peace in her soul.

She wanted to make her own way, earn her own keep—stand on her own two feet, rather than sail on the family's wealth or hide in plain sight on the back of a horse.

'I'm going to be Carmen de Luca in America,' she told her brothers.

'You're going to use *her* name...?' Sebastián frowned. 'But you hate her!'

'Perhaps. But I'll use her name if it buys me a chance of freedom.'

'But you love riding…' Alejandro still insisted.

Did she, though?

Her passion for horses had been fully indulged, yet not a soul knew or understood that at first riding had simply been her one true rebellion…

Carmen had been just a little girl, standing at the top of the stairs, eavesdropping as her *papá* spoke on the phone with her *mamá*. Her heart had started to thump with excitement as she'd heard them discussing her…

'Flamenco lessons?' Papá said. 'She's only four!'

Carmen felt giddy with excitement as she pushed the door of her mother's studio open.

Her mother had abandoned the studio, just as she had abandoned her children, yet Carmen often sneaked in. There was the scent of Mamá in the air, even if Carmen couldn't remember her. There were shawls and castanets and shoes with nails in the heels and toes.

Sometimes she would drape a shawl around her shoulders and push her little feet into the shoes, or tie a faded silk rose into her long dark hair and smile at her plump little body in the mirrored walls. She had painted her lips red once, and her cheeks too, and put on a pretty bead necklace.

Sebastián, who had been a teenager then, had washed the lipstick off her face…

'But I want to dance like Mamá,' she had told him.

After all, Mamá was a world-famous flamenco dancer. She had seen her—and not just in the photos that lined the studio walls and the bar over at the bodega. Carmen had heard her mother's rich voice giving interviews on the radio, and seen her on television. She had even heard her mamá say to a reporter how it broke her heart to be separated from her children.

The reporter had asked if she might one day perform with her daughter. Mamá hadn't answered that question. Instead she had spoken about the devotion that the art of flamenco required. Still, Carmen's little mind had lit up with visions of her on the stage beside her famous and beautiful mamá...

She would be a mini Maria de Luca, and Mamá would scoop her up into adoring arms.

And now Mamá was coming home to teach her.

Carmen's heart soared as Papá came off the phone.

'Mamá has seen the photos I sent her of you. She thinks you're too...' He paused and sounded sad. 'She wants you to start flamenco lessons.'

'Yes!' She jumped up and down in excitement and delight. 'When? When can I start?'

'Soon. I will call Eva.'

'Eva?' Carmen had blinked. Eva was a flamenco dancer who came to the exclusive infant school that she attended, and gave private lessons to some of the children. 'But Mamá is much better than Eva.'

It was that night that she had begun to comprehend that her *mamá* had no intention of coming back.

Yes, Carmen was needy and demanding. And she had screamed that night for her mother, over and over. It wasn't her father, or her brothers, nor Paula, her nanny, she wanted.

'Quiero mi mama!'

I want my mummy!

When it had become evident her *mamá* wasn't coming—was never coming—Carmen had chopped off all her long black hair, right there in the studio. And on the day of her first private flamenco lesson Carmen had refused to come out of her bedroom.

'Carmen,' her papá had sighed, weary from the antics of his overly dramatic daughter. 'Mamá thinks you need more exercise.'

'I don't want to dance flamenco, like Maria.' It was the first time Carmen had called her mother that. 'I want to ride horses.'

Even at five it had felt like revenge when she'd won her first ribbon. Her father had laughed at his daughter's apparent fearlessness. In truth, Carmen had been terrified.

She still was, at times, but she would never let anyone see it.

Even though Papá had been proud of her achievements, he had been so depressed, so desperate for his wife's return, that he had just thrown money at the situation rather than offer true guidance.

It was Alejandro who had told her to stop holding out any hope that Maria might one day return, and Sebastián who had had 'the talk' with her about periods. *They* were the ones who had guided her in place of her parents.

And now it was her brothers who were telling her she needed to fight.

'Papá wasn't in his right mind when he made his will,' Alejandro said as they walked back towards the cars.

'He was never in his right mind where Maria was concerned.' Carmen shrugged.

'Perhaps,' Alejandro agreed, 'but he always said this was to be your home.'

Papá *had* said that.

It was clear that this legal dispute had nothing to do with money. This property, the land, were small change in the grand scheme of things.

'This was our home…' Alejandro said as they came to the sweeping driveway.

Carmen could see the pain in his features, knew that the agony of their childhood wasn't solely hers.

Sebastián was less sentimental. 'She had nothing to do with Papá until she discovered he was dying, and she hasn't been near the place in twenty-five years.'

Perhaps he caught Carmen's awkward swallow, or noticed that she'd turned away from her brother's gaze.

'Is there something you're not telling me?'

'Of course not.'

'Because if we do fight her, then it will all come out in court.'

He levelled a shrewd stare at his sister, but Carmen looked away and stood silent as he carried on speaking.

'Fair enough. I get that you need a change of scene. Just don't rush into anything. I'm going to speak with Dante.'

The Romeros really did have everything: Capitán Dante was the captain of Sebastián's luxury yacht.

'He'll organise a leaving party for you. Anna and Emily will want to see you before you leave.'

'Of course.'

Carmen nodded and kissed Sebastián on the cheek, then watched him walk towards the car. She wished Alejandro would leave with him.

'Carmen,' Alejandro said. 'What's going on?'

'I just miss Papá so much…'

'I know.'

'I feel as if I let him down…'

Her *papá* had always said he wanted to see her married, to walk her down the aisle. But she had balked at the men her father had deemed suitable, or she had tried dating them only for it to end in disaster. Carmen knew she had intimacy issues, and was so terrified of rejection that she simply did not know how to let anyone get close.

And then there had been the endless rows that had soured the time she'd had left with her father following his diagnosis. She had loathed how he had taken back their mother, and how he had continued to defend her and explain away her actions. And now, in Carmen's name, the Romero siblings wanted to dispute their father's will…

'I don't know if I want to fight,' Carmen admitted, wondering where all the anger she'd once nurtured had gone. 'Alejandro, what if she's changed—?'

'Carmen!' he interrupted swiftly. 'You know better than that.'

'Of course. But what if she really wants to come back here…?'

She saw his expression and halted. Of her two brothers, she had thought Alejandro would be the one who might just understand. Despite everything that had happened, the child inside Carmen still wanted to believe her mother had changed, wanted to give her this chance to prove it…

But, no. 'Do not go soft on her now,' Alejandro warned her darkly.

Carmen felt his words like a knife in her heart. Something inside her had changed since her father's death, and she feared that maybe Alejandro was right: she *was* going soft. In fact, scared that she was weakening, she had, unbeknownst to her brothers, already booked her flight.

She was leaving for LA tonight. No sentimental goodbye party on a yacht for her!

She felt it was imperative that she get away as soon as possible.

Alejandro and Emily would soon be taking their baby daughter, little Josefa, on a trip to England. What if they decided to remain there?

Sebastián and Anna were already planning an extended trip on the yacht to celebrate their new family as soon as Willow's adoption came through.

And now her father was gone...

At any moment Maria might return to her beloved flamenco, leaving them again, just as she had all those years ago.

People hurt her or they left. Carmen knew that only too well.

That was what they did.

She didn't want to fight any more. Not for a house and land...not to be loved. She was just too tired. Too heartsick. Alejandro was right. She *was* going soft.

But from this day forward, Carmen vowed, she would *always* be the first to leave...

CHAPTER ONE

Elias Henley had attended more awards nights than most movie stars.

Tonight he stood, seemingly relaxed and poised, with Wanda, his regular date for such events, by his side.

His thick brown hair was superbly trimmed, his chiselled jaw freshly shaven, his tuxedo immaculate. He looked every inch the Hollywood heartthrob—for surely someone that good-looking must be famous!

But the glances and whispers as onlookers tried to place him came only from those not in the know.

Those in the know treated him with a certain reverence.

After all, the barrel of his burnished Namiki pen might as well be filled with liquid twenty-four-carat gold, such was the value of Elias Henley's signature.

Yet, whether or not you were in the know, one constant remained: Elias Henley was something of an enigma.

His exquisite face had not been touched by needles, and his hair—including the flash of silver—was all his. The combination afforded him a distinguished edge. Even the slight receding at his temples only made him sexier, unique as it was in this setting. There were real lines at the corners of his eyes, and his brow actually furrowed to indicate emotion…

It did so now.

'Hey, Elias.'

A movie producer came up and shook his hand and suitable small talk was made. Or rather, Elias made small talk. The producer, desperate for news of any progress on the finance he wanted for a script, couldn't hide his impatience.

'I was just talking with your father about—'

'I'm surprised you could find him…' Elias quickly deflected the talk away from the project the producer wanted to discuss and looked over his shoulder. 'Ah, there he is.'

He looked towards his father, William Henley, who was in his utter element, relishing the buzz of the event, while his mother, Eleanor, stood quietly by his side, nodding and smiling.

Tonight was an exclusive event, at which his late grandfather's movie financing company would be recognised and undoubtedly rewarded. For now, though, it was a drinks reception—an opportunity for networking and everything Elias hated.

He intended to leave most of the speeches to his father, who excelled on nights such as these. But there was, though, one speech that Elias was expected to make.

It was the one night a year he detested more than anything else: the occasion when the Henleys would be announcing the recipient of an award named after their late son—a full-ride scholarship to study film at the Californian college many of his successful family had attended.

Elias would thank everyone for their donations and reiterate just how much this scholarship would change the life of its lucky recipient. Then he would acknowledge Seraphina, his late brother's widow, and how hard she worked alongside his mother to make this award a success.

And, despite his seemingly unruffled demeanour, Elias was dreading it.

He stood, utterly unmoved, as the producer reiterated

the wonders of the script upon which Elias was about to undertake a full risk assessment.

'It's a guaranteed winner,' he emphasised, assuming they were the words Elias wanted to hear.

But the man was preaching to the wrong choir. Elias was sick of guaranteed winners, and his father's preference for movies that played it safe.

'We'll be in touch,' Elias said, in a voice that indicated the conversation was over.

He remained unmoved as the producer shuffled off.

'You can be so brusque!' Wanda hissed. 'I wanted a chance to talk to him. You could at least have introduced me. What *is* your problem tonight?'

Where do I start? Elias thought, as he saw that Seraphina and her husband Vincent now stood conversing with his parents.

He would like to be able to say, after all these years, that he wished her well.

But he did not.

It was then that he noticed the slight swell of her stomach beneath her gold dress, and recalled observing Vincent's team toasting and congratulating him a couple of weeks back. While he and Vincent might now be on opposing polo teams, they were old friends...

Elias glanced towards his mother, who was smiling and immaculate, but he knew the strain she was under tonight. Elias hoped, if he was right, that Seraphina and Vincent wouldn't share their happy news just yet. Elias would prefer to break the news to his mother in private. Not that she'd betray any emotion other than sheer delight. But even so, Elias knew the news would hurt her.

Although he looked impressively immaculate, tall and elegant in his tux, and was conversing politely with all and sundry, there was a restlessness to him that made him something of an enigma. He might look the part of red carpet idol, but he would rather be riding—either women or horses.

But he couldn't be described as a playboy—because at thirty-five he was no boy, and he certainly didn't play.

Well, he played polo, but he took that extremely seriously. His current team was relatively new, but they were already making waves...

'Elias?'

He frowned as he saw Seraphina making her way towards him. It was only then that he realised Wanda had seized her chance and was now talking to the producer he'd so recently snubbed.

'On your own tonight?' Seraphina observed, while taking a glass of champagne from a waitress.

Perhaps she wasn't pregnant after all...

Elias stared into her cold blue eyes and her pretty china doll face.

'Go to hell,' he told the woman he loathed.

'I just miss you so much,' she said urgently. 'There isn't a day when I—'

'Do you want me to state it more loudly?' he fired back, his voice low with enough threat that she heeded his warning and walked off.

'Sorry, darling...'

Wanda was back, and she reached out a hand to rearrange his tie, but in a reflex gesture Elias arched his neck and turned his head away.

He *loathed* unnecessary touch.

'If we were a real couple,' Wanda drawled, removing her hand and taking a drink from the proffered tray, 'then the occasional display of affection would be expected.'

'Wanda, if we *were* a real couple,' Elias responded

tartly, 'then you'd know by now that I abhor feigned affection and—'

Elias's irritation was abruptly halted as he saw the ghost of a smile on the waitress's full lips.

He wasn't remotely embarrassed that a waitress might have overheard his conversation—hell, this was LA. Everyone gathered here tonight surely knew that he and Wanda were not a couple. She was his date for functions such as these, but no more than that.

Elias Henley was close to no one by choice.

He kept his relationships superficial at best, and with good reason—he didn't trust anyone and nor did he want to.

His arrangement with Wanda benefited them both: he required a beautiful woman on his arm, and she made the most of his network of contacts to further her career in the movie business.

As for sex—it was a basic need. But he wasn't fulfilling it with Wanda.

The waitress's subtle smile remained on her face, and it surprised Elias, for staff at such a prestigious event usually knew better than to eavesdrop quite so obviously.

He lifted his brown eyes to meet her almond-shaped black ones.

She didn't blush, nor drop her gaze, and nor did she swiftly move on. 'Would you care for champagne?' she offered, in a rich Spanish accent.

He gave a curt shake of his head. Really, given there were staff milling about everywhere, there no need for her to offer. If he wanted a glass of champagne he merely had to reach out for any passing silver tray.

'No, thank you,' Elias said, and turned back to his date.

He frowned, surprised that Wanda didn't appear to have

even noticed the waitress—neither her faintly mocking smile nor how she'd hovered...

It was a non-event.

A fleeting moment that should instantly have been forgotten.

And yet Elias found he dwelt on that subtle smile.

It had felt almost as if she shared his attitude towards nights such as this.

And the rich Spanish edge to her voice lingered in his mind even as Wanda asked, 'Have you prepared your speech?'

'No need.' Elias gave a tense shrug. 'It's the same speech I've been delivering for five years now.'

The first year—eight months after the death of his twin—Elias had wished for the glare of a harsh spotlight in his eyes so he could not see the faces looking back at him as he delivered his speech.

His father must have dropped twenty pounds, Elias had thought that night, looking at his unusually gaunt features. His mother, as always, had been immaculate, with pearls at her ears and throat, yet he'd known the supreme effort it had taken for her to attend.

There had been a hush, an air of tense expectancy, for it was the first time anyone from the family had spoken publicly of Joel's sudden and tragic death.

His throat had felt so tight...as if there had been hands around his neck, squeezing, squeezing, *squeezing*...

Elias Henley, who rarely broke a sweat except when he was riding, had felt a cold trickle down his spine and icy shards piercing his temples.

Thanks to a privileged education, he'd been used to public speaking, and had already been holding his own in the family business. Life hadn't been perfect, though, not even before his brother died. He'd felt pressure to dedicate himself to the long-established family business—had felt the tightening of its constraints pulling him into the world of movie finance even as his heart drew him towards polo and horses...

It had been nothing he couldn't handle, though. And then...

Elias reached for a glass of water, rather than champagne, to clear his head and ease his tight throat. He found he was curiously disappointed that it was a different waitress who held the tray.

He wasn't nervous about the speech. Oh, no, his mood tonight was far more dangerous than that.

Elias was angrier than he usually dared to be on a night such as this.

Despite appearances...despite what everyone thought... his seemingly perfect life hadn't ended on the night of his brother's death.

It had ended a couple of weeks before.

'Your father's coming over,' Wanda warned him.

'Yep.'

'A quick word, Elias?' William Henley's smile disappeared as he spoke to his son. 'Your mother might be playing it down, but the foundation's board members have made it clear that if we want the award to continue in its full capacity—'

'I'm well aware,' Elias cut in.

He was more than aware of the financial situation of the foundation. He'd made a huge anonymous donation himself—and not for altruistic reasons. He didn't want his mother to find out that the donors' interest was waning.

'People want more than just the same old cursory speech. Say how much you miss him, or—'

'I've already been well briefed by PR,' Elias snapped.

'If you don't want to talk about yourself...' William

gestured with his hand, as if plucking ideas from the air '…then talk about the wedding. Talk about how happy Joel and Seraphina were.'

'That would hardly be fair to her current husband,' Elias replied tartly.

William Henley blew out a tense breath. 'Talk about the last five years, then. How you've dealt with grief. How you've found the strength to move on…'

Perhaps at that moment William saw the flash of warning in his son's eyes, because he took a second to regroup and then played his trump card.

'The award means everything to your mother.'

'I know it does.'

His father screwed his eyes closed in frustration. 'Give them *something*, for God's sake!'

He didn't outright call his son a cold-hearted bastard, but the implication was very much there.

'Would it kill you to show some emotion or to say how you're feeling?'

As Elias's father stalked off, Wanda chimed in with some acting advice. 'Fake it if you have to,' she told him. 'I can give you some pointers.'

Elias pressed his lips together to mask his fury.

There was nothing fake about his emotions.

He was holding them in. He had been holding them in for five years now. If he let them out… If he dared open that box…

Be careful what you wish for, he thought, as he watched his father return to his mother's side.

The reception was over and the guests were being ushered in for the meal, which would be interspersed with awards. It was always a long and tedious night, but at least soon it would be over for another year.

Elias was thinking of Domitian, a problem stallion he'd

recently acquired. The beast would be missing his evening gallop along the beach, and so too was he. Blake, his yard manager was on a day off, and there was no one else who could or even would ride him.

'Elias!' Wanda whispered, pulling his focus back to the ceremony—he saw they were waiting for desserts to come out. 'Would you please get me a lunch or something with that producer?'

Elias knew he was being appalling company tonight, so he nodded, which quickly cheered Wanda up.

'Do you know what I do when I want to look as if I'm upset?' she ventured.

'No.'

This evening could not be over soon enough, Elias thought, his mind drifting as Wanda talked at length about the acting tricks she used to express certain emotions. His only saving grace came as he was watching the desserts being brought out.

There was the mystery waitress.

She was no longer smiling. Her apron was twisted and she was carrying only two small plates, while the other servers were carrying three or four. Her previously neatly tied back hair had begun to unravel, and there was a dark flush to her cheeks.

'Are you listening, Elias?'

He wasn't, and he felt bad at how little attention he had paid Wanda this evening, so he turned to her and forced himself to focus.

There were a lot of awards…

Films backed by Henley Finance scooped up more than their share—as they did most years.

The company Elias's grandfather had founded was still flourishing.

'Look at all these, Elias. Do you really want to leave?' his father said, gesturing to the awards that littered the table.

Elias gritted his jaw. The conversation he'd had with his father, and later his mother, about possibly leaving the company had been a private one.

'Leave?' Seraphina perked up at this snippet of information.

'Those damn polo ponies!' William huffed.

'Vincent's team is doing really well.' Seraphina squeezed her husband's arm. 'I think they'll take the cup.'

She smiled over at Elias, but it only made the bile churn in his stomach.

'It might be your team against Vincent's in the final…'

'Elias?' his mother prompted. 'Seraphina's talking to you.'

'I think I'm about to be called to speak,' Elias said, grateful for the usher who came over and told him he was indeed needed to make his way to the stage. 'Excuse me.'

The audience were undoubtedly expecting the usual polished performance. It was five years now since Joel had died, and Elias had delivered a variation of the same speech every time.

Elias thanked the sponsors and the donors and all the people who had made the award possible. Then he spoke briefly about the selection process and the quality of candidates who had competed to win the scholarship.

He looked to his father, who sat holding his mother's hand. She'd been a much sought-after interior designer before Joel died, and had overseen the impressive refurbishment of Elias's Malibu ranch.

It was the last project she'd undertaken, though, and she had since refused his repeated requests for her help with the restoration of the grooms' lodge. Instead, she had devoted herself to this scholarship, in a bid to keep the perfect memory of her son alive.

With the formalities out of the way, Elias looked out at the now rather bored audience and knew his father was right. Public interest in the scholarship was waning, and he couldn't bear to see his mother's heart broken all over again.

He knew he could do more. *Should* do more…

'After Joel died,' Elias said, in his deep, measured voice, 'it was as if my world stopped turning…'

He moved his tongue over dry lips, unable to tell anyone, let alone an audience of people he cared nothing for, that he'd been lost.

'I moved out of LA in an attempt to get my bearings. And I guess I've never quite made it back…'

He glanced at the audience and it was clear that his attempt to describe, even obliquely, how he'd felt was not going down well. This was his chance to do what his father had suggested.

'People often ask how I dealt with my grief. Joel and I were not only best friends…we worked together, socialised together, played sport together… Well, we did until he fell in love with my mother's new assistant…'

He forced out a smile to indicate that he'd just delivered a good-natured little joke, and glanced towards his family's table, at his late brother's seemingly sweet widow, who was clutching his mother's other hand…

'A few months before Joel died we celebrated his marriage.' He could not bring himself to say Seraphina's name, he realised. 'He was the happiest I've ever—'

Elias swallowed audibly. He attempted to continue, to give the audience what his father claimed they clamoured for, but his mouth was dry…so dry. He was so burdened with the weight of the truth, so weighed down by the secret only he and one other person knew, that suddenly he did not think he could keep the lid on that box of emotions for one second longer.

Because Joel had *not* been happy…

And now, as he stood in front of the podium, attempting to articulate the depth of his loss, all Elias could feel was the same abhorrence and disgust he had felt two weeks before his brother had died.

The sheer disbelief when Seraphina had attempted to kiss him.

Pushing her off, Elias had said two words that no gentleman should ever say to a lady.

Oh, but she was no lady.

'It's you, Elias,' Seraphina had sobbed, *still* reaching for him, *still* trying to kiss him. 'It's always been you… Joel doesn't have to know.'

'You *disgust* me.'

She still did. And there was no one he could tell…

Or could he?

There were awkward coughs from the impatient audience.

He glanced at his father.

You want feelings? How about I tell everyone what Joel was really doing on his cell phone when he died? How about I tell them that he was driving and sobbing, asking me if he was going mad or if his new wife had gone cold on him…? Why don't I tell them how it felt to lie to my twin and tell him he was just imagining things? Why don't I describe that brief sense of relief I felt as Joel laughed on the other end of the phone, and agreed with my rallying words?

'You're right,' he said. 'It can't be a honeymoon every day, can it? You won't tell anyone?'

'Joel,' Elias replied. *'Do you even have to ask? Of course I would never tell anyone.'*

'Thanks.'

'Give it time,' Elias had said to his brother.

But there had been no more time.

Not for Joel.

Elias had heard Joel's sudden shout of alarm, then a horn blaring and the screech of brakes.

He recalled it now so vividly that he could almost smell the burning rubber...

He hadn't experienced a second of relief ever since.

As he stood at the podium, he felt as if the smoke from the wreck was choking him, filling his nostrils and making his eyes smart.

'On the night my brother died, he called me.'

It was information only those close to the family could possibly know. He looked straight at Seraphina, and he loathed that she had the nerve to look back at him, that she had no idea how close he was to telling all those present what had really occurred.

Nothing had occurred, Elias reminded himself.

But only because of him.

Had it been up to Seraphina...

'Joel had a question for me,' he went on. 'He wanted to know how come his new wife...'

Elias watched her rapid blinking. Perhaps she had begun to sense just how out of control the usually measured and emotionless Elias Henley currently was.

'He wanted to know—'

CHAPTER TWO

'DE LUCA!'

Carmen was certainly not listening to the boring speeches. Even if she was supposed to be as invisible as a ghost, there was still a lot of work to be done.

This was her third job since arriving in America, and she desperately wanted to hold on to this one. *Had* to hold on to this one if she was to keep her promise to herself and not use Romero money.

But it was hard to be treated so badly. And not just by guests: it was the treatment of staff by the owners and managers that had caused her temper to rise until she exploded.

She glanced over to the manager, who nodded towards a table where someone was signalling for more wine. Carmen made her way over with an ice bucket.

The lady shook her head. 'I asked for sparkling water.'

'Of course,' Carmen said, and went and collected the necessary bottle.

But as she started to pour she heard the current speaker—or rather, heard the uncomfortable pause.

Looking over to the stage, she saw that the speaker was the man from before.

He was too good-looking not to recall.

He'd made her smile earlier, with his honest response to his partner.

It had been no more than that.

But now she could see that he was in trouble.

Carmen was more than used to this type of function—had been to a thousand such events herself. Albeit usually she was seated rather than serving. Still, she was aware—as was everyone else in the room—that this pause in the smooth proceedings had gone on for too long.

The man's brown hair gleamed and his stunning features were amplified by the lighting. He wore his evening suit exceptionally well, and yet despite the excellent cut of the fabric he seemed somehow confined.

Carmen watched as he reached up to adjust his tie, but then changed his mind and awkwardly brought his hand back down to his side.

Was he nervous? she pondered briefly. But why? Perhaps he had forgotten the name of the person receiving whatever award he was presenting?

But now she was really watching—and she saw that he was *not* nervous. He reminded her a little of Sebastián on the day of their father's funeral, attempting to be civil but having to bite his tongue and keep a lid on his deep and complex emotions.

She knew that look.

This speaker was struggling to contain himself…

His hands were clutching the podium, his breathing was shallow, and his eyes were shooting daggers into the audience…

There were three things that hauled Elias back from the brink.

The promise he had made to his brother when he'd identified his body—that no one would ever know about his wife's vile betrayal.

The fact that Elias had sworn to protect his family—especially his mother—from further hurt.

And the sudden distraction near the back of the room, which gave Elias an easy excuse for his extended silence...

'Hey!' the lady cried, as the water Carmen had been pouring spilled over the top of the glass and quickly pooled across the table.

'I'm so sorry!' Carmen offered,

But the woman leapt up, knocking her chair over, furious that her dress was wet.

'I'm drenched!' she shouted into the awkward silence.

'Ma'am, I'm...' Carmen took a breath and reminded herself that she was working.

She hoped to God that she had never spoken to a waitress like that. No. She might be spoiled and difficult, but only with the people she loved.

She clamped her lips shut on the retort she wanted to make, that the woman's dress was barely wet. 'I do apologise, ma'am.'

The manager ran over, followed by a troop of waiters with cloths, but all Carmen was really aware of was that the speaker had found his voice.

As the small commotion at the back of the room faded he apologised for the interruption, checked that he could progress, and said, 'Yes, Joel asked me how come his new wife and he were so fortunate...'

'De Luca!' her manager hissed. 'I'll speak to you in the kitchen. *Now!*'

All eyes must be on the speaker, of course, and yet Carmen felt as if every eye was on her... She was going to be fired, she knew, and she blushed as she made her way between the tables.

As she reached the swing doors to the staff area the speaker was concluding his remarks.

His voice reached her.

'I've been asked, many times, "How do you deal with grief?"'

Carmen, who had been desperate to escape, now found she paused to hear his answer.

The weight of her own grief was unbearable.

Worse even than the day her *papá* had died.

She did not know how to deal with it, and was desperate for answers.

Please, Mr Good-Looking, Carmen thought, *tell me it gets better. Tell me how to deal with this ache in my soul...*

'Five years on...' she heard the slight husk to his tone '...I still don't know the answer.'

His words brought no comfort.

None at all.

She pushed through the swing doors to face her manager.

'De Luca!'

Her boss was awful.

Horrible.

'What the hell were you thinking?' He was right in her face. 'Only, you *weren't* thinking, were you?'

'It was a simple accident,' Carmen said. 'And I apologised immediately.'

'You've been here for a week and there's a disaster every night.'

'I spilt some water. I don't see the issue.'

'I'll tell you the issue...'

And he proceeded to do so, just as he had every night this week.

Carmen had to bite her tongue, so tempted to pull off

the apron of this stupid outfit the female waiting staff were made to wear and tell him where he could stick his job.

That was exactly what she'd done at her last job.

And the one before.

She'd pulled rank, told them what they could do with their attitude, and said that if that was the way they treated staff, no wonder they couldn't keep them.

Her fiery nature was returning, she realised, but then she checked herself. Tonight she *would* hold her tongue.

'I am *so* sorry,' Carmen repeated.

'Not good enough.'

He really let her have it then, telling her that she was going to have her wages cut...

They clearly thought she was an illegal worker. That had been the assumption in all the casual jobs she had gone for.

Carmen loathed the way the workers here were being treated.

She looked over at the junior chef, who stood, head down, listening to the manager's tirade. She knew the chef wanted to leap to her defence, but he had a family to support.

She looked at another waitress, Joni, who she knew was trying so hard to stay on the straight and narrow and keep a regular job.

It wasn't just Carmen's fiery nature that was returning, but a deep hatred for injustice that was starting to emerge.

'Do you know why you can't keep staff for more than five minutes?'

Carmen hadn't got where she was in the equestrian world by staying quiet—there she was able to speak her mind, and she would do the same here. She could not keep her silence.

'Because you're a disgrace!' Her lips curled in contempt. 'You berate and you bully!' She spoke for everyone here, because she was the only one who could afford to. 'You take wages and you steal tips!'

'Now, you listen to me—'

'No! I will not!' Carmen shook her head. 'You're going to listen to *me*. I would never speak to my staff the way you do—and I make sure my staff are properly paid. You've held back thousands of dollars in tips in just the week I've been here.'

She told him the amount exactly, and watched the manager's nervous blink.

'How many staff are working tonight?' she demanded.

Nobody responded.

'Very well…' Carmen did the maths herself. 'I think that works out to about one hundred and ten dollars each are owed. Including the staff who are absent tonight.'

'Get out!' he told her.

'You don't know who you are dealing with. I'm not going anywhere until all these staff are paid. Failing that, I'll be reporting you…'

Carmen's tirade built up steam as she listed the authorities she'd be contacting, and then repeated it to the owner of the venue, who had been alerted to the commotion and had come to see what the problem was.

Carmen named the law firm her family used for their professional dealings in LA—the same firm that had swiftly sorted out her temporary work visa.

'I can call them now and get the police to come too… report you for breaking labour laws…' She took out her phone and quickly pulled up her contact at the law firm, to show she meant business. 'Up to you?' Carmen warned.

And finally they conceded.

Carmen stood, arms folded, until all the correct tips were dispersed.

'Take your job…' now she pulled off her apron and

tossed it onto the floor '…and your stinking attitude, and shove them. And if I hear there are any repercussions, or that this practice continues, I shall be making several calls. I've got my eye on you.'

Joni was in tears as she followed Carmen out of the back entrance. 'You've no idea how much this means…'

Carmen was starting to. Even though she had grown up a long way from this kind of situation.

'Call me if this nonsense starts again. I'll make sure they won't find out it's you,' she said, and she hugged Joni.

As she stepped out into the night Carmen felt sad rather than proud. She had wanted to make her own way not only as a matter of pride, but because she had wanted to prove to herself that she could do it.

She'd thought coming to LA would give her a new sense of purpose, fix her somehow, or at least make her feel better. Instead, she felt lonelier than ever, and even more lost than the night she'd boarded the plane.

There had been more than a kernel of truth in the manager's words, Carmen reluctantly acknowledged. She was a truly dreadful waitress.

She crossed the strip and took a long look back at the hotel where she'd hoped to somehow prove herself, find herself…but then she did a double take when she saw him.

Him.

He was outside the main entrance of the hotel, where people were milling about and talking. He had stepped aside, away from the bright forecourt lights, and he cut a solitary figure, leaning against the wall, looking out at nothing.

There was something about his stance that stopped Carmen mid-stride.

He looked as if he might be having as wretched a night as she was.

More so, perhaps.

He had made use of the distraction of her water-pouring disaster to explain the momentary lapse in his sleek delivery, but Carmen knew damn well the true order of events.

Her spilling the water had not been the cause.

Yet, there was somehow an effect.

Suddenly he looked over. And she no longer felt like an invisible ghost because he was staring right at her.

Perhaps she should have quickly looked away, but instead she raised her hand and tapped her forehead with the side of her forefinger. It was a Spanish gesture that indicated *fed up to here*, but she realised it must look as if she was saluting him, or something equally bizarre…

But he just smiled. Clearly he'd understood her meaning, because he copied her gesture—he was fed up to *here* too.

She watched as he pushed himself off the wall and straightened his jacket, before strolling confidently back inside as Carmen headed off to catch her bus.

Of course she could order a cab, but there was that little matter of personal pride…

Surely she could last three months without using Romero money? Carmen asked herself when she arrived back at the tiny soulless apartment she had taken on a week-to-week lease. God, she wanted to order food in. But, reminding herself she couldn't afford it, instead she poured a bowl of cereal.

She scrolled listlessly through the job vacancies on her phone, and knew that tomorrow she'd be doing the rounds of restaurants and—

Something caught her eye.

Yard Manager

She read the job description. It was a permanent role, managing a stable.

No.

Hadn't she come here to have a break from horses?

But it was then that it dawned on Carmen that this break from horses had taught her precisely how very much she missed them.

Bowl of cereal forgotten, Carmen scrolled eagerly through various other jobs.

Stable hand... Casual position... Immediate start... Polo experience preferred...

Well, she didn't have any experience of polo, but when she saw the yard was in Malibu, Carmen read on.

Early starts... One day off a fortnight during polo season...

Carmen smiled, because that didn't concern her at all. She knew what that wording *really* meant: must love horses.

And she did.

She really did.

At the age of twenty-six, with a successful equestrian career, it should have been a given, but Carmen had never been free of the nagging suspicion that she only rode because it was a way of getting back at her mother.

But she *did* love horses. So, so much.

A stable hand?

No pressure.

No need to perform in the incredibly highly skilled art of equestrian ballet.

No management responsibilities.

She could just put her head down and get on with it...

Excitement bubbled in her for the first time since Papá had died.

Malibu!

The hills, the oceans, the horses...

Surely there she would be able to find herself?

Carmen de Luca, stable hand.

Why not?

CHAPTER THREE

'YOU HAVE *NO* experience with polo?'

'None.' Carmen shook her head as she walked through the impressive stables with Blake, the yard manager. 'But I have worked with dancing horses.'

'Dancing horses?' Blake gave a slight, almost derisive laugh, perhaps thinking her heavy Spanish accent meant she had chosen the wrong word. 'You mean dressage?'

'Well, yes, that too, but…' She shrugged, remembering that she didn't want to reveal the extent of her real skills or experience. 'Sort of…'

'It doesn't matter,' Blake said. 'We need someone to stay back on game day. We've got a couple of mares in foal, as well as—'

He halted their conversation and called out to one of the grooms to stop letting the horses out.

'Domitian is out,' he said, and then explained what he'd meant to Carmen. 'We have a stallion causing problems. He's usually taken out later in the day, but Elias wanted him to expend some energy before the vet examines him.'

He stopped discussing the stallion and got on with listing the duties Carmen would be expected to carry out.

'Exercising, cooling, settling…'

Carmen hadn't planned to do any riding on her working holiday, so hadn't brought her gear. In keeping with her attempt at budgeting she wore some dreadful brown cotton trousers she'd found in a thrift store, as well as scruffy second-hand Cuban-heeled boots that were just a little too big. She had topped off the look with her favourite T-shirt from home, which was navy and had boldly written across the chest *NO BAILO*. As always, she had on dark leather gloves—her biggest expense as she'd had to buy them new. Her hair was pulled back in a low ponytail and her whole look was such that she was glad there weren't any mirrors around the stable yard.

Furthermore, she had spent a *lot* of hours sitting at a bus stop, so she could arrive fifteen minutes before the start of her early-morning interview ready to prove herself.

Strangely, apart from downplaying her experience of competing and stable management, she felt she was finally being herself—her true and honest self.

So determined was she to get this job that she had packed up her things and given notice on the apartment, knowing they wanted someone who could start immediately. She hoped her backpack indicated as much to the yard manager.

It wasn't her scruffy attire that was the issue, though. He was clearly in doubt as to her ability to manage these very expensive and tempestuous horses.

'You'd be…what…all of a hundred pounds?'

Perhaps the equestrian world was the only one where you could get away with asking someone their weight at a job interview, but just then a rider came into the yard on a steaming black stallion and Carmen acknowledged that Blake's question was possibly merited.

Blake greeted the rider. 'Hey, Elias, how was he?'

'Guess,' came the surly response.

That single word demanded her sudden attention. Because Carmen looked up from the magnificent horse, snorting and blowing, and saw who the rider was.

It was the man from the other night! From the hotel ballroom! Carmen was incredibly grateful that he was too focused on containing the stallion even to notice her.

So, his name was Elias.

And she simply knew that he owned the place.

It was clearly a busy yard, so the interview was being cobbled in between its normal activities, and Carmen took absolutely no offence that she was being ignored. If anything, she welcomed it, for as Blake updated the owner with details about a mare in foal she was able to fight her blush by turning her attention to the stunning stallion.

She was doing her best to dismiss the brief interaction they had shared the other night.

Why did it matter? Carmen pondered.

But that was the moment—at six in the morning in a stable yard in Malibu—that a little bit more of what was missing in her life returned. The other night was forgotten and all her worries drifted away as the stallion sniffed the air in her direction and made his first curious approach.

'Hola, caballo,' she said gently, introducing herself.

He breathed out softly, then moved his head a little closer as he breathed in her scent again, and Carmen took it as a polite greeting. Instinctively, she slowly extended her closed hand to greet him.

'Hola, guapo,' she murmured—*Hello, handsome.*

But before his gorgeous nostrils could make contact, Elias jerked back on the reins.

'Watch it!' Elias barked.

Carmen snatched back her hand, aching to touch the horse. She was about to register a brief protest and point out that mutual contact had been about to be made, but then she saw Elias's dark brown eyes narrowed in warning.

She reminded herself that this was not her yard, and these were not her horses.

Here, by her choice, she did not make the rules.

There was also an inward sense of relief that, as evidenced by his clear lack of interest, Elias hadn't recognised her.

Why it should matter, Carmen didn't really know. She would examine that later. But for now, while she was being interviewed, it simply came as a relief.

It was Blake who explained to her the nature of the beast.

'Dom's a vicious bastard,' he informed her, and glanced at her leather gloves. 'Those won't protect you—he's a biter, amongst other things,' he added, although the last sardonic comment was aimed at Elias. 'Apart from me, Laura's the only one who'll take his feed in. Elias, I'm just interviewing this girl for the stable hand position. No experience with polo and she'd only be a hundred pounds soaking wet…'

'Not a girl,' Carmen corrected. 'And I am one hundred and ten pounds.' Then she added, 'Dry.'

This was the world she was used to—because, far from taking offence, Blake grinned.

Elias did not, however. His jaw seemed to be moulded from granite, Carmen thought as she spoke on. 'As well as that, I'd have no issues feeding him.'

She looked up at Elias but he made no response—at least not to Carmen.

'Let's get him cooled down,' he said, and Blake held Domitian's bridle and reins as Elias dismounted lithely, his long black boots thudding onto the ground. The familiar sound made Carmen jolt with sudden longing, but he paid no heed to her jump, his attention solely on the hot and bothered horse.

Domitian—or Dom—was more aggressive without his rider, she thought, but Elias and Blake took up positions on either side of the stallion's head and together led the unwilling horse into the stable.

Elias held him while Blake hosed him down, although Domitian proved something of a moving target. Carmen stood there feeling rather useless as she watched both men get drenched.

'Can I help?' she asked—and not just because she was still being interviewed. It was more that she simply wanted to be a part of the action again.

Elias was having none of it, though. 'You can help by staying back,' he called over his shoulder, then took the hose from Blake and finished off the horse's neck.

Carmen smiled as he let Domitian chase the hose and take a drink. 'You like that…?' he crooned, and Carmen saw the ghost of a smile on Elias's stern features as he let Domitian play for a couple of moments, biting at the water rather than at people. Then it was time to take him to his stall.

Everyone seemed to be staying well back from the stallion, Carmen noted—all the staff scattered as the stallion was moved through the stable. They were clearly nervous—and with good reason. His tail was swishing and he kept trying to lurch towards the other stabled horses as they passed the various stalls.

It took both men to steer him straight, but finally he was in. If it were her horse, Carmen thought, she would not have housed him in the last stall, where he had to pass all the rest of the horses to be moved in or out.

She was so used to making such decisions that it was going to be hard to hold her tongue.

'Blake!' someone called out, and she was told to 'wait there' as he headed off to do whatever he needed to.

Carmen stood there, feeling redundant, as the yard came to life and the grooms started to let the horses out and the day got underway.

It felt pleasingly familiar to be there, yet frustrating to stand idle and not be a part of it.

She thought not just of her own yard, and of how Presumir would be whinnying and calling out for attention if she was left to stand still doing nothing, but also of the busy mornings she'd spent at the famed equestrian school in Jerez, which had been such a big part of her life.

By now she'd be out riding, or would have just returned, breathless, from taking the most difficult of the mounts out. Or perhaps she would be sipping a well-earned coffee with colleagues and friends before starting schooling or rehearsing for the famous shows. Sometimes she taught a class—never beginners, but riders who had travelled from all across the globe to learn from masters of the art of equestrian ballet...

For six weeks Carmen had told herself that she didn't miss it...that after twenty-two years of riding, she needed time away from the horses...

Now she was trying to fathom how she'd survived so much time apart from them.

She wanted to be the one dealing with Domitian.

She watched as Elias exited the stable, pleased to note that he didn't close the door, thereby letting the horse know he was the boss. When Domitian's black nose appeared, Elias didn't hold a stick, or use the flag that was pinned next to the stable door, but instead lifted an arm and pointed, telling him firmly to get back. Domitian clearly complied, because she heard a snort and the nose disappeared.

Elias stood patiently, refusing to bolt the door closed and walk away until he had control of their relationship.

He ran his hand through tousled hair. It had been sleek and brushed back from his face the other night, but it was now black and shining from sweat. His white jodhpurs and black polo shirt were drenched, though how much was exertion and how much was from hosing down the restless horse she wasn't sure.

'Elias?' a female voice shouted. 'Your father's on a video call. He wants you there…'

'Tell him I'm busy,' Elias said, still not closing the stable door.

'I already have,' she called back. 'He says they'll wait.'

'Great…' he muttered under his breath.

Carmen looked over and saw a silver-haired, middle-aged woman poking her head out of the office.

'Give him this,' she said, and threw a bundle to Carmen, who caught it.

She realised it was a towel wrapped around a shirt. A business shirt…

Was she supposed to hand them to him?

Elias wasn't paying attention to her. He was still focused on Domitian, but it was clear the horse was staying well back in the stable.

'Do you want me to feed him now?' Carmen offered. 'While he's back?'

He briefly glanced over. 'You're not to go in with him until Blake or I give the all clear.'

Carmen shrugged. 'Here.' She tossed him the bundle and he caught it.

'Thank you.'

Not *thanks*, as was more commonly used here. For a brief second—*very* brief—she felt his eyes on her, and she recalled that he'd been one of the very few guests at the event the other night to thank her.

For the first time she wondered if perhaps he did, after

all, recall her, but then he turned back to Domitian, who was still behaving and staying well back in his stall, despite the other horses being moved through the yard.

Though Elias was sweaty and dishevelled, and still a touch breathless, he looked somehow more at ease than he had the other night. And, to Carmen, ridiculously more handsome—if that were possible. He had been dressed in the finest tailoring then, and yet the jodhpurs showed off long, muscular thighs and taut buttocks.

Just when Carmen was about to look away, Elias made it impossible for her to do so—because he pulled off his drenched top.

Carmen worked with sports people all the time, and was more than used to well-exercised and toned bodies—professionally, a body was simply a vehicle, a machine to be fed, exercised and maintained. Personally, she'd dated all the men her father had approved of, and had spent a lot of time on the beach or at parties, sometimes aboard Sebastián's yacht. She was usually surrounded by a plethora of men who perfected their bodies solely to be seen, or to impress, or to provoke a reaction...

Usually they did not. Not in her.

Carmen had started to wonder if she was actually *capable* of reacting in that way...but now she saw Elias's honey-brown torso and his dark chest hair. She watched him dry himself as he continued to focus on Domitian, warning him now and then to move back and letting him know who was in charge.

He dried his flat stomach, and the curly black hair there, then held the towel in both hands and ran it across his back.

Goodness, he was stunning!

In all the usual ways, but also in ways that were inexplicable to Carmen.

Why did the flat mole on his left shoulder look as if

an artist had chosen to place it there? Why did the raising of his arm to warn Domitian to move back, and the glimpse of dark underarm hair, make her feel as she was being pinched between the tops of her thighs? And why did the glint of an expensive watch on his wrist make her think not of its obvious value but instead of him taking it off at night?

These were not the kind of thoughts Carmen was used to. Not at all! So much so that she was ridiculously grateful that her thrift shop boots were a size too big, for there was room for her to curl her toes.

Thankfully, he pulled on his shirt.

Thankfully, because even if hiding away such a vision of male beauty felt akin to closing the shutters on a stunning sunrise, Carmen seemed to have forgotten how to breathe.

He was tucking in his shirt when he glanced over at her, as if suddenly aware of her attention. Carmen had to quickly come up with something to say. 'Your father...' she mumbled. 'He's waiting.'

'So he is.'

He closed up the stable, then headed off.

'Laura?' he called to someone who now stood behind Carmen—the same woman who had thrown her the clothes. 'Make sure Domitian moves to the back of the stall when you feed him.'

'Sure,' Laura said and, holding a bucket of feed, Carmen watched as she took down the flag to wave at the stallion to get it back.

Laura was a little tentative, but actually good with him, but of course Carmen would have done things differently.

Carmen closed her eyes.

I am a stable hand!

It was her new mantra.

She was here to do the grunt work, not run the yard…
She could do that with her eyes closed.

As Laura carried on with her duties, Carmen wandered closer and looked at the many posters tacked to Dom's stable.

STAY BACK!
I BITE!
AUTHORISED EMPLOYEES ONLY

'Those signs are there for a reason…'

She jumped when she heard Elias's voice and swung around.

'I was just admiring him,' Carmen said. 'I thought you had a meeting.'

'It's done.' He refused to meet her eyes. 'Blake's been called away and he's asked that I show you around.'

'I'm sure I can find my way…muck in where needed…'

'This isn't a farm,' he said in a snobbish voice. 'Or some backwater riding school.'

Carmen really had to bite her tongue and stop herself from telling this arrogant man just who was…

She repeated her mantra in her head. *I am a stable hand…*

'Let's get started…'

CHAPTER FOUR

It was clear to Carmen that Elias was reluctant to play guide, but she took no insult. Certainly, she hadn't been expecting the owner to give a new stable hand a tour, but it was obvious something unexpected had happened with Blake, and the yard was a busy one.

'Laura would usually step in—' he nodded to the silver-haired woman '—but she's with the farrier this morning. Laura's our head groom.'

'Hey!' Laura looked up from the horse's leg she was holding and gave Carmen a welcoming smile, then spoke to Elias. 'I'll take over as soon as I can, but if I can't get there she'll be in the attic.'

'The attic?' Carmen asked, but he offered no explanation.

Instead, he asked, 'How many can you take out in a set?'

'A set' was riding one horse and leading the others in order to exercise them.

'Four,' Carmen said. 'Five if I know them.'

'Start with three.'

Clearly he wasn't prepared to take her word. It was fair enough; she wouldn't take on a new hire without observing them at work either.

Next, she was shown the office, which boasted a huge electronic board for updating feed rations and vitamins and such, as well as a scruffy desk. She glanced through a door and blinked at the rather unexpected sight of an additional office that looked better suited to a glamorous city high-rise than a horse yard, no matter how well-heeled.

'Yours, I presume?' she said.

In response to her question he closed the door, making it clear to Carmen that there was much about this man that was off-limits.

Completely off-limits.

Elias had been thinking about the dark-haired beauty since Saturday night—not just their brief exchange outside the venue, but also the subtle smile she'd imparted and her throaty voice as she'd offered him champagne.

It was rare that his mind dwelt on someone like this. He'd trained himself to be impervious to charm—and not just at work. He kept himself distant when it came to sexual partners too.

Riding into the yard, he had recognised her immediately. Dom had been startled at the sudden tension evident in his rider.

Elias had been less than thrilled to find that Blake, who dealt with all the hiring decisions, had already decided to take her on for the position.

'She seems great,' Blake had said during their brief exchange in the office.

'A bit overly confident,' Elias had suggested, but then halted himself—because there was no tangible reason he could call upon that justified why she shouldn't be hired.

There was one intangible one, though: a silent allure.

Oh, yes, he certainly remembered her from the other night.

How could he forget her smile, or the distraction she

had caused that had snapped him back to attention, saving him from revealing too much in his speech.

And then there was that moment when he'd stepped outside for air...

It had nothing to do with preferring not to be attracted to a stable hand—it wasn't him being a snob. Elias didn't want to be that attracted to anyone. He didn't even want to be that *aware* of anyone.

Ever.

And he'd been aware of her before he'd so much as met her black eyes. That smile had been enough to draw his gaze upwards...

'I'll put her through her paces on Rocky when I get back,' Blake had said. 'She can only do six weeks, but it gives us time to find someone permanent. After the Martin debacle, I want to take my time and get it right.'

Elias had nodded his agreement. Even though he usually left the hiring and firing to Blake, he'd fired the last stable hand himself.

'You don't mind showing her around?' Blake had checked. 'Erin called, and I do need to go and see her...'

'What about Laura?'

'She's with the farrier. Do you want me to—?'

'It's fine,' Elias had cut in, as if it were no trouble at all.

And now, those dark eyes bored into his back as he picked up a couple of apples and showed her around the yard.

'Most of the horses are out, or waiting for their turn,' he explained.

It was clear to Carmen that his brisk stride was familiar to the animals, because heads came over the stable doors to greet him.

'This is Winnie.' He took an apple and gave it to her.

'She's our top pony. I generally ride her in the first and fourth chukka.'

'I'm completely lost,' Carmen admitted. 'I have no idea what a chukka is.' She couldn't help adding, 'And that's not a pony. She's a horse.'

'Yes, but in polo they're all called ponies,' he explained.

They moved swiftly on past several empty stables. 'You can check they've been fed on the board in the main office, or on here—' he pointed to the tablet beside each stable '—and make sure you update the record or they'll end up being fed twice.'

'Sure.'

'It's not complicated…' he let out a tense breath, '…you just swipe here…'

Carmen suppressed a smile as her impatient teacher showed her how to use a tablet as if she'd never seen one before.

'I think I can manage,' she said. 'But *thank you* for your patience in explaining all this technology to me.'

He looked at her, unsure whether it was merely her rich accent and throaty words that had made her tone seem as if it was laced with sarcasm. And then, of course, there was that smile again—not as obvious as it had been on Saturday night, but there all the same.

'I'll take you in to meet Capricorn,' Elias said, to cover his sudden and unexpected awkwardness.

His march to the next stable had begun, but Carmen didn't rush to follow him. Instead, she gazed up at the magnificent high ceilings and the purpose-built yard that would be any horse-owner's dream.

'What's down there?' she asked.

But she was speaking to thin air, for he had already gone into the stable.

'This is Capricorn,' he said, stroking the neck of a beautiful grey thoroughbred mare who was clearly in foal.

The vet who was with her was taking out some equipment.

'Come over,' Elias invited Carmen. 'If you work here you'll be spending a lot of time with her.'

'Hola, mi belleza,' she said as she approached and, unlike when she'd introduced herself to Dom, and put out a gentle hand, she was not warned to step back.

The mare sniffed the air, and as her velvet nostrils pushed past Carmen's gloves and met the skin of her wrist Carmen almost wept. It had been six weeks of no horses, and for Carmen it suddenly felt as if she'd had six weeks of no sustenance, no food, no contact…

'She's restless,' Elias told the vet as Carmen fussed over her. 'She's not settling at night. Just doesn't want to lie down.'

'Bored?' the vet suggested. 'Perhaps she hates missing out on game day.'

The vet examined her for signs of foaling, but there were none, so he listened for a long time to her heart rate, and that of the foal.

'I'm worried about sleep deprivation,' Elias said. 'She's jumpy…'

'How long does she have to go?' Carmen asked.

'Eight weeks,' the vet responded.

'Is she a maiden?' Carmen asked, and the vet glanced over.

So too did Elias. Capricorn, like some first-time pregnant mares, did not appear to be as advanced as she actually was. Clearly Carmen knew her stuff, but what had

Elias frowning in slight bemusement was that the vet, who was generally a man of few words, responded to her readily.

'She is, and though she's hiding it well the foal's a good size.' He carried on talking about position and size, answering all of Carmen's intelligent questions.

Elias could not quite work out what was happening, nor could he hide his increased bemusement at the exchange. Of course the staff often liaised with the vet, and treatments were discussed amongst the team, but this was more than that. There was a certain arrogance to this stable hand—a confidence and a level of experience not quite fitting with someone applying for such a casual role.

And clearly he wasn't the only one who'd noticed—the vet was opening up like a California poppy to the morning sun.

'Capricorn used to be the star here,' the vet explained, 'but then she went lame. She's obviously bored, though, so some gentle walking might do her good?' he suggested. 'Perhaps try her on the water treadmill.'

'She's not keen,' Elias said. 'Thanks to that bastard—'

'Who?' Carmen asked, but he ignored her question. 'What about taking her down to the beach?' she suggested. 'It would be easy on her joints.'

'For sure,' the vet agreed. 'Win-win.' He nodded to Elias. 'Right, let's see Dom, then.'

Carmen was left outside the stable for that consultation, and amused herself by scrolling through her phone, looking at new pictures of little Josefa and reading about the upcoming Jerez Horse Fair.

It would be the first time since her childhood that she'd missed it. Her heart twisted when she thought of the Romero marquee, where her father and brothers would invite favoured guests—the golden ticket that everyone wanted.

Carmen had usually managed to escape that part—she'd always been too busy at Horse Fair time to attend corporate events and had thankfully been excused. She'd stop by, though—briefly—and her father would smile in delight and introduce her and her beloved horse Presumir, who would be beautifully groomed and looking her best—

'Carmen!'

She looked up and from his impatient stance realised it mustn't be the first time Elias had called her name.

'If you can drag yourself away from your phone, go and saddle up Winnie.'

'Sure.'

'She kicks,' he warned.

'You're giving her Winnie to try out on?' Laura checked, frowning at Elias as they walked past. 'She can be a bit feisty.'

'Good,' Carmen said. 'So can I.'

Unfortunately for Elias, Carmen handled Winnie brilliantly.

So much so that he decided he'd be asking the vet to give his favourite polo pony a once-over—because his usually temperamental mare, who loathed anyone riding her except him, was as docile as a lamb and followed every one of Carmen's instructions.

Damn, she rode like a dream!

For once he wasn't admiring the horse, but the rider. And there was a smile on Carmen's flushed face when, having watched her put the mare through her paces, Elias could not find a single fault.

'Where did you work before?' he asked.

'An event venue in LA.'

Elias refused even to blink. 'I meant what stables did you work at?'

'A few places back home in Spain…'

Carmen wasn't the first casual worker to be evasive.

'A riding school… I have my own horse there… I went through all this with Blake.'

'But you have *no* polo experience?'

'As I said to Blake, none.'

Carmen was smiling on the inside. She knew the job *had* to be hers after the way she had handled Winnie.

And she was not wrong, because with Winnie stabled, and after a glance over to Laura, who was still stuck with the farrier, Elias said, 'I'll show you where you'll be staying.'

On the way, he pointed out the old riding school and arena.

'It's next to the vet and therapy facilities. We'll probably move Capricorn there soon, but I don't want any unsettling changes for her right now.'

'Your place is gorgeous,' Carmen said, smiling. 'The old riding school reminds me of where I had my first lessons.'

But he clearly wasn't hanging around to hear about that, and she had to run to keep up with him.

They went past the immaculate polo lawn only used on game day, then the practice fields and schooling arenas, and finally, after a morning of seeing the very best of the best, they came to a tall wooden building that had definitely seen better days.

'The front door doesn't work,' he said, and took her around the back, where there was a large covered summer kitchen.

'Everyone takes it in turns to cook,' Elias explained,

scrubbing out what must be her predecessor's name from the chalkboard. 'But I'm sure they'll let you off tonight.'

'I would hope so,' Carmen said, with a flutter of panic erupting in her chest as she realised that she would have to cater for everyone on Mondays.

'I'm sure Laura can better explain. I know they usually make enough for lunch the next day too. Go ahead—' he gestured to a rather flimsy door '—take a look around. I think Laura said you were to have the attic.'

'Aren't you going to show me around?'

'I'm sure you can find your way,' he responded tartly. 'Attics are usually at the top...'

He felt her scowl, and knew it was deserved, but Elias could not face going in there. He stood in the bright morning sun and thought he really didn't care if his tour guide rating would suffer as a result. He hadn't set foot in the place for five years. Not since the night Seraphina had—

He absolutely would not be taking Carmen up the stairs to the attic.

Elias stood there, frozen to the spot, trying not to recall coming out of the bathroom, a towel wrapped around his waist, unaware that Seraphina was planning on betraying her new husband with his own twin...

He felt the churn of bile in his stomach as he couldn't help but remember aggressively wiping from his lips the taste of lipstick that had transferred to his mouth when she'd tried to kiss him. When he had recovered from his shock—at first incredulous, then furious—he'd packed up his things, and had been in the process of departing when Seraphina had confronted him again.

He'd been telling his sister-in-law *exactly* what he thought of her just as Laura had come through the door.

'Where are you going in such a hurry?' she'd asked.

'I'm moving out while the bathrooms are being renovated,' he'd said, and had watched Laura's expression change as Seraphina had come down the stairs behind him...

The slam of a door brought him back to the present, and he saw Carmen walking towards him—a welcome distraction from the darkness of his memories.

Elias glanced at his watch. 'I have to head into work.' He saw her frown and explained, 'My other office is in LA.'

'Oh.' She glanced at his attire. 'You're going into the city dressed like that?'

He smiled rather than give an answer—a real smile—and she saw his beautiful teeth. It made Carmen feel all lit up inside...

'Laura will sort you out with a yard uniform.'

'Er...not so fast,' Carmen said, halting him before he could walk off. 'Am I being offered the job?'

'I'll leave the official offer to Blake, but yes.'

'You should have saved some of those posters from Dom's stable to nail to *this* door!' Carmen half joked.

'Excuse me?'

'The whole building should be condemned.' She looked at him challengingly. 'It's a dump.'

'I'm sorry if the *free* board and accommodation isn't up to your usual standard,' he clipped, and then added sarcastically, 'It would seem I've wasted your morning.'

'You haven't,' Carmen said, not remotely perturbed by his haughtiness. 'I'd love to accept the job. But I'm unable to start until tomorrow.'

He didn't so much as blink—just pressed his lips together as she spoke on.

'If I'm expected to sleep here tonight I'll need to clean

the bedroom—and also the bathroom.' She looked around the summer kitchen doubtfully. 'As well as in here.'

Elias had *never* met anyone like her. She was tiny—like a little Jack Russell that didn't know its own size, or rather couldn't care less. But, dammit, in this instance he knew she was right. The place had been a dump even five years ago...

'There's no need for that. I'll call my housekeeper and have her send some staff over.'

'Good,' Carmen said. 'And could you ask that she brings fresh linen? I don't believe my predecessor changed the sheets.'

'Fine. I assume you're accepting the position?'

'I am,' Carmen said, and then swallowed. 'Thank you for the opportunity.'

'You're so welcome,' he responded, and gave her a saccharine smile.

But before he headed off Elias knew there was something else that had to be said.

'One more thing...' He looked right at her. 'We need to address the other night.'

Carmen felt the breath still in her lungs. She had honestly thought he hadn't recognised her, or that he'd forgotten. But then again, how could he have? They had stared at each other, assessed each other, just as they were doing now...

'What about it?' Carmen asked.

'I keep my LA life very separate from my life here.'

She guessed he was referring to his date and the conversations she'd overheard.

'At least, I do my level best to do so.'

'I signed an NDA when I was employed by the venue,' Carmen informed him. 'So don't worry—your secrets are safe...' She looked at him. 'Whatever they may be.' She shrugged, as if she couldn't even remember what had been said. 'Do you have any more questions?'

'Just the one.' He glanced down at her T-shirt and then met her eyes again. 'What does "NO BAILO" mean?'

It was the Californian sun hitting her face that set her cheeks on fire, surely? The sun and a fractured night spent at the bus stop, to ensure she made the early-morning interview. That was what had her feeling a little *altered*...

It could not be the feeling of his eyes dusting her body and then returning to her gaze.

Nor could it be the memory of his naked torso this morning...

It was the sun, Carmen told herself. Because it couldn't be anything else.

She'd never known anything else.

And so she dragged her mind back to the question.

'It means,' Carmen said, somehow still holding his gaze, 'that I don't dance.'

Though Elias nodded, there was something in his eyes that told her he believed otherwise...

And there was something about Elias that made Carmen *feel* otherwise...

She pondered that as she watched him walk away.

CHAPTER FIVE

'PAELLA!' CARMEN SAID confidently that evening, when asked what she would cook for them all next Monday.

She even wrote it by her name on the chalkboard.

For tonight, though, it was pizza for all and getting to know the new girl—and, of course, talking about the yard.

Actually, it was mainly talking about the yard.

Carmen was more than used to that, and very happy to eat pizza and glean what she could.

'What did the vet say about Dom?' asked John, one of the ten or so grooms who lived in the lodge. 'Did anyone hear?'

'Gelding…' Laura responded.

'The sooner the better.'

'Even if it's done tomorrow it will still take months for him to calm down,' Laura sighed. 'Elias wants to put some more work in on him first. He's still hoping to sire him.'

'Well, *I'm* not going near him again.' John shook his head. 'That leaves you feeding him, and Blake and Elias riding him. What the hell's Elias going to do with him if it doesn't work out? He can hardly join the Misfits.'

'Misfits?' Carmen checked.

'The horses that end up on Elias's property,' Laura said, laughing. 'They're not exactly the elite.'

'That's putting it mildly.' John rolled his eyes. 'Dom

would finish them off in five minutes. I know Blake's had enough of him.'

'Where *is* Blake?' Carmen asked.

'He's got a cottage in the grounds.'

'Well, hopefully it's nicer than here...'

'You've surely seen worse,' Laura said, and Carmen quickly remembered that perhaps, as a young stable hand, she *should* have seen worse.

'Maybe...' Carmen shrugged, but then thought of her own yard. *Her* staff would walk out in protest if she offered them this accommodation. 'Elias doesn't seem to mind spending money on his horses or himself...'

Carmen had glimpsed his sprawling ranch house from the tiny attic, and after six weeks of dreadful bosses she refused to be a slavish devotee—as Laura clearly was.

'The wages are good, and there's no set budget for food like there was with the last owner...' She took another slice of pizza, as if making a point. 'Elias is great.'

'Only because he didn't kick you out when he found you sleeping rough in the barn!' John threw in.

'True...' Laura shrugged and then explained things to Carmen. 'I'd lost my job at the riding school. Well, I had a go at the owner about his training methods.'

It was nice being amongst people who spoke her language again, Carmen thought. To talk about horses and not much else. Although her ears did pick up when Elias was mentioned again.

'Anyway,' Laura continued, still defending her boss, 'Elias doesn't ask us to do anything he wouldn't do himself. He lived here while the ranch was being renovated.'

'For five minutes,' John retorted. 'He took one look at the place and moved to a luxury hotel!'

'No, that was only when Seraphina—' Laura bit down

on whatever she'd been about to say. 'He only moved because they were about to start ripping out the bathrooms.'

'Well, the renovations never happened.'

'Because Joel died,' Laura snapped, and stood up. 'I'm on settling duty.'

'I'll come with you,' Carmen offered. 'I'll be doing it myself soon.'

'Ignore John,' Laura told her as they walked towards the yard. 'He thinks I have a crush on Elias.'

'Do you?' Carmen smiled.

'Of course!' Laura laughed. 'Everyone does!'

The yard felt different in the evening. Perhaps it was calmer because Dom was out, and most of the horses were resting. Not Capricorn, though; the pregnant mare was pacing.

'I tried her on the treadmill this afternoon,' Laura said. 'Without water, but she hated it.'

'Why not take her to the beach?' Carmen asked. 'The vet said it was fine.'

'When do I have time to do that?' Laura pointed out. 'It might be easier now you're here. Martin was her main carer.' She glanced over at Carmen. 'Elias fired him.'

'For...?' Carmen asked as Laura tried to soothe Capricorn.

'Capricorn hates the water level on the treadmill going past her hooves, but Elias caught him filling it up just to upset her.'

No wonder Elias had been less than polite when he'd spoken about Martin to the vet.

'I'll take her for a walk on the beach and then settle her,' Carmen said. 'You go to bed.'

'It's your first night...'

'Honestly, I'd love it. It will be nice to get my bearings.'

Laura showed her the track to the beach, and Carmen led the very tense mare down towards it.

'You're okay,' she crooned to her new charge, deciding that Elias was right to be worried about her. 'You need to sleep at night if you're going to have a baby,' she told her, but her words faded as she saw that Elias was on the beach with Dom.

'What *is* it with him?' Carmen asked her charge.

What was it with her? Elias thought as Dom galloped him through the waves and he saw Capricorn walking the shoreline alongside Carmen.

To see one of the grooms walking a horse certainly wasn't an unusual sight—there was nothing nicer than salt water and the ocean, and he could see how relaxed Capricorn appeared, for once... Yet as he pulled Dom into a walk, he didn't do it solely to avoid unsettling the restive mare.

Elias didn't like the way he'd spoken to Carmen this morning, and how it might have soured relations with his newest stable hand. With his head clearer now, thanks to the ride, he wanted to put that right.

'Hey...' he said as he approached.

'She was tense and pacing,' Carmen said. 'I thought a walk might help her.'

'She loves the beach.' He looked at Carmen. 'Thank you.'

'For what?' She smiled at the glorious setting sun. 'It's not as if it's a hardship. You live in a beautiful part of the world.'

'Yes.'

He dismounted and walked the stallion alongside Capricorn. 'How's the lodge looking?'

Though she clearly wasn't about to worship at his feet for providing the basics, she did push out a smile.

'It's better. You have a wonderful housekeeper.'

At first their conversation was awkward, but then she asked him about the upcoming polo semi-finals.

'You're a new team, yes?' she said.

'Three years now.'

'Do you think you have a chance?'

'Absolutely.' Elias nodded assuredly. 'At least that's what I'm telling the team.'

'What's the truth?' Carmen asked.

Nobody got close to his truth.

But Domitian, for once, was relaxed—so much so that he was simply walking, instead of trying to mount poor Capricorn as he usually would.

There was only the beautiful Malibu night, and surely there was no threat in her question.

'We haven't a hope!' He half laughed. 'I can't believe we've even made it to the semi-finals. But if we do win, there's a chance we'll be playing my old team in the final.'

'Are there bad feelings?'

'No, nothing like that… Both my brother and I used to play for them. Mind you, it was more of a hobby for him.'

Elias fell silent then, because there was a deeper truth—one he would *not* be sharing—which was that there was a part of him that didn't even want to make the final.

He still hadn't told his mother that Seraphina was pregnant, but more than that he loathed the fact that, if the two teams did meet in the finals, then *she* would be there—again—with his family. Needling her way in…giving him that seemingly sweet smile that turned his stomach…batting her eyelashes over innocent blue eyes as if she'd completely forgotten how she'd come on to him…

How she *still* came on to him.

Elias knew it was some sort of perverse and twisted game that she was playing, but he had long since given up attempting to work her out.

Certainly, there was no one he could discuss it with.

He'd always been guarded with his feelings, but since Joel's death he trusted no one but himself with the truth. In any case, he wouldn't be discussing such matters with the new stable hand!

With anyone.

'I'd better get Dom back...' He nodded in the direction of the yard.

'Sure,' Carmen said. 'See you tomorrow.'

'No.' He shook his head. 'I'm in the office tomorrow.'

She was squinting in the low sun, and as she put her hand over her eyes he registered her frown.

'LA,' he said.

'Oh, you mean your real job?'

'That's the one.'

'Well, good luck... I guess.'

Elias had left by the time she returned to the yard, and Capricorn, tired from her walk, settled easily.

Just as Carmen slipped her bolt and went to leave, she changed her mind and walked down to the last stall in the row.

She looked at all the warnings posted on Dom's stable—and promptly ignored them.

She did not look directly at the stallion, just spoke gently, quietly pleased when he made his confident way over and snorted at her. And then, just as she'd wanted him to that morning, he sniffed her outstretched hand.

Blake was right. If he was going to bite her, gloves wouldn't help much, so she slipped one off.

'*Ah, mi guapo. Eres amable?*' she asked softly of the handsome animal.

Her question—whether he was going to be gentle—resulted in a puff of air being blown onto her skin. She moved to stroke his nose.

It seemed he was indeed going to be gentle with her.

'What happened to you?' she asked, wishing, as she so often did, that horses could simply tell her.

She felt his velvet nose and his hot breath, and then he dropped his muzzle down so she could stroke his face. She chuckled and told him a secret.

'I think I am more scared of your boss than I am of you...' Carmen whispered.

Or rather, she was scared of these new and unfamiliar feelings.

The wonderful thing about talking with horses here was that she could do it in her native Spanish, so nobody around her would understand. She could pour her heart out to them and they would stand calmly as she did so, accepting her whispered confidences.

Dom was no different, standing quietly as she told him about her day.

'I'm sure he thinks I grew up in some barn, with a couple of old horses and donkeys!' she said, and laughed.

Don nudged her hand, wanting more attention.

'Are you looking for a treat?' she asked, and for the first time looked directly into his dark brown eyes. 'Good boy,' she said, stroking him, reassuring him that this eye contact wasn't a challenge.

Dom was true black, with not a single white marking that Carmen could see. He was absolutely beautiful and, yes, he would be an incredible sire.

'I don't blame him for not wanting to give up on you,' she told him.

There would be a lot of work required, though, and even then it might not work. Sadly, some animals could not be fixed. Schooling the stallion, riding him, trying to gain the trust and respect he had clearly lost somewhere, would be the only way.

Elias was completely right—no one should be near him unless they had serious experience.

But Carmen *was* seriously experienced.

And maybe, just maybe, she could work with Dom...

Of course, neither Blake nor Elias would ever agree, unless she revealed to them her true skills...

No!

Instantly, she discarded that idea. She was here to discover herself—not to return to being the old frightened and confused Carmen Romero...

'Tomorrow,' Carmen told the gorgeous stallion, 'I am going to bring you a treat.'

She had bought some hand-made liquorice for Presumir, as a present—it was the only treat she ever used for training...

'And I'm going to make you my project.'

After all, taming an aggressive stallion seemed a far safer bet than falling for the boss.

CHAPTER SIX

FOR THE MOST PART the world felt a little more as if it was in the correct order now that she was back working with horses again.

Each morning Carmen woke on a very uncomfortable mattress to the sounds of Laura and John making out in the bedroom below—though apart from that she'd never have known they were a couple.

When they were finished—and fortunately it was always very quick—Carmen would pull on the yard uniform of cream jodhpurs and the same kind of black polo shirt that Elias wore. Then she would go to the bathroom, brush her teeth and tie back her hair, and then head down the creaky stairs to stand in the outdoor kitchen, gulping coffee with the others as the lunches were handed out.

Lunch was usually leftovers from the previous evening's dinner, in a wrap, as well as fruit and yoghurt or something similar.

Generally by the time they got to the yard Dom had already been ridden, or they'd stand around waiting for him to get back.

'Elias should just get it done,' John would moan, and a few others would agree that Dom was a hopeless case.

Yet Carmen knew different.

She was slipping him treats, even going into his sta-

ble at times, and Dom was beginning to give her space…
to let her move around him without startling or reacting.

This morning she was taking out Winnie and two others, trailing Laura who, as always, had her earbuds in.
Sometimes Carmen would overtake her, because she loved
these mornings, cantering along a stretch of flat, then
walking up a long track lined with trees and eventually
emerging into sunlight that painted the sky lilac, lavender
and then blue. It always took her breath away.

Carmen trotted on, loving the sound of the joyous snorting the animals made as they stretched their legs. She
passed other sets and felt her heart rate lifting as she relaxed into the moment. For the first time since her father's
death she felt as if she could fully breathe—as if her lungs
were filling again after being crushed inside her chest for
too long.

LA had been lonely. She was used to her brothers, family and friends, and had loved life until her mother had
returned.

Actually, that wasn't true, she acknowledged.

She pulled on the reins and slowed the set to a walk as
they looked down at the valley.

Carmen knew she had never truly been at peace…

She'd never truly fitted in…

Some of her 'friends', Carmen knew, liked her only for
the invitations to Romero functions—like the parties that
had used to be held on her brother's yacht—and Carmen
always paid for lunch or dinner… As for family… While
she loved her brothers, she wished they would stop pushing her to become close with their new wives.

She'd even had a row with Sebastián a couple of weeks
before she'd left.

'Would Anna really love you if you weren't a Romero?'

Carmen had asked, in her oh-so-direct way. 'Seriously, would she?'

'Do you know what, Carmen?' her brother had said. 'She loves me *in spite* of it.' He had glared at his sister. 'We're not exactly a welcoming lot.'

Yet, despite her inner turmoil, on this beautiful hazy Malibu morning Carmen felt she was starting to know peace.

'How did I ever think I needed a break from you?' she asked the animals she was getting to know.

She breathed in their earthy scent and felt the cool shade of the forest, waving to Laura, who had turned now to head back, racing with John along the flat.

Then, as it did most mornings, her mind flicked to Elias...

Laura's easy admission that everyone had a crush on Elias had made her smile, and yet for Carmen it was such an unfamiliar sensation.

He was the first man to have sparked her interest since her move to America. In fact, if she were being honest with herself, she had to admit that he was the first man she had *ever* been truly attracted to.

Carmen huffed out a breath and turned her set for home.

She had been on many dates, all vetted by her *papá* or her brothers, that had bored her to tears. She'd been out with a few with guys she knew they didn't approve of too... But she had never once experienced true attraction—that feeling when you actually ached at the sight of his bare skin, or when a mole upon a shoulder became a memory...

She was done with men, Carmen reminded herself, taking out her cell phone.

Laura listened to podcasts as she rode, and some of the others listened to books or music, but Carmen made use of the time difference and often caught up with family as she rode, knowing it was afternoon back in Jerez.

'How's America?' Alejandro asked this morning, and they chatted away in Spanish for a while.

'Better now I'm back with horses.'

'I knew you'd miss them. How is it being a stable hand?'

'Frustrating at times, but mostly I love it.' She told him about her secret work with Dom. 'If the boss decides to geld him I'm blowing my cover and buying him. I want him to sire Presumir...'

They were chatting about little Josefa as Carmen approached the yard.

'Emily sent you some videos,' Alejandro was saying.

'Yes, I meant to message and say thank you.'

'Please do!'

She heard the slight edge to her brother's tone. 'I am working, Alejandro. And I'm very busy. As well as that, I have to cook for everyone tonight.'

'God help them.'

'Do you know how to make paella?' she asked.

'Easy,' Alejandro said. 'You call the chef and say you would like paella.'

That did make her laugh, but her smile was soon wiped off her face as he turned the conversation to Elias.

'I've just been looking up your new boss, Carmen. Steer clear,' he warned. 'He has a worse reputation than I used to...'

'*Lo dudo!*' she joked. *I doubt it.*

She shrugged and laughed again as she guided Winnie into the yard and dismounted, nodding her thanks to John, who took two of the set from her.

'Believe me,' Alejandro said, 'he's even worse than Sebastián was. From what I can tell, he has a regular date for functions, but—'

'I don't need details,' Carmen interrupted. Did she halt him so abruptly because she knew that already, or because it stung? 'Anyway, he's hardly going to look at a stable hand.'

'True!' Alejandro laughed. 'Still, even if he knew who you were it wouldn't make much difference. I don't think it's conversation he's after...'

Elias wasn't after anything. In fact, he was actively avoiding the new stable hand—or trying to—but Carmen seemed to be everywhere.

The team adored her—possibly because she was one of the few people bold enough to feed Domitian. Elias had called her out on it a couple of times, when he'd seen her coming out of the stallion's stable. He'd been discomfited to notice that the flag the staff generally used to get him to stay back was still hanging by the door.

'What are you doing?' he'd demanded.

'Feeding Dom,' she'd responded.

'You're supposed to just put the bucket down and get out.'

'Don't you like a bit of conversation with your dinner?' Carmen had asked. 'Does your maid just put down your food, wave a flag in your face and leave?'

There was an air of insolence about her, and he couldn't help but like it—especially when it caused her to shoot him a daring look from under her brows.

And this morning he saw that look again.

His warning to Blake had been right—she was overly confident, blithely chatting away on her phone as she gave Winnie a light tap on her rump to guide her into her stable.

Elias had no choice but to call her out on it.

'Carmen!' He strode over. 'Be more careful,' he warned. 'Don't forget they kick.'

* * *

'Donkeys kick,' Carmen said, laughing.

She closed up Winnie's stable and returned to her conversation with Alejandro as she turned to go and check on Capricorn.

But it would seem Elias hadn't got her joke.

'Carmen!' he said. 'Could you get off your cell phone when I'm talking to you?'

'I'd better go,' she said to her brother in Spanish.

'He has no idea of the fire he's playing with,' Alejandro said, and laughed, clearly enjoying the exchange. *'Luego.'*

Carmen didn't respond—not to Alejandro nor to Elias—but she pocketed her phone at least.

Elias, however, had not finished.

'What does that even mean?' he demanded. 'Donkeys kick?'

'It was a joke.' She shrugged, barely looking up as she checked Capricorn over.

'Not a very funny one,' Elias said. 'Winnie's not some little pony at a riding school. You need to be more aware.'

'I am always aware.'

Carmen knew her retort was a little smart, but she was doing her level best not to blush. In truth, she was far too aware of Elias Henley, but determined not to show it.

She did not like playboys, and had already guessed that Elias was one—even before Alejandro had rather crudely confirmed it.

The last thing she wanted was to be blushing around Elias, because he would sense it, she knew...

'I don't want any of my staff injured through carelessness.'

She felt her lips become almost pinched, and it was as though lemon juice had pooled in her mouth, as she laboured to restrain herself from giving a smart answer.

'I am never careless, sir,' she said. 'But I take your warning. Thank you.'

'Good. I'm bringing out Dom in a moment.'

'Sure,' Carmen said, and then poked her tongue out as he walked off.

She saw his back stiffen, as if he knew what she had just done.

He turned back, and she gave him a butter-wouldn't-melt smile.

Elias didn't return it. 'Is there a problem, Carmen?'

'Not really.' She shrugged. 'Maybe a bit…'

She pinched her lips again, reminding herself that Elias was the owner and she was but a lowly stable hand. But Carmen was very used to asserting herself and not having to justify her actions—especially around horses.

'I was just speaking with my—' She snapped her mouth closed, remembering she was supposed to be refusing to explain herself to him, but then she found she couldn't help herself. 'It feels a lot like…'

Seeing his features tighten, she was sensible enough to stop then.

'Go on,' he invited, his dark eyes still holding hers.

Though she could not be certain, she felt as if he was daring her to continue.

'Say what you were going to say.'

Very well!

'Am I at school?' Carmen asked, and watched his eyebrows rise. 'Because that was the last time I was told off for using my cell phone. I *do* know my way around horses, and I'm confident—'

She did not get to finish.

'There's a difference between confidence and arrogance,' he told her.

She almost laughed at the irony as he pointed his finger. Possibly he saw it too, because he halted the gesture.

'So, in future, get off your damn cell phone when you're in the yard—especially when I'm about to bring Dom out.'

He turned on his booted heel and she turned towards Capricorn.

'Yuck!' she said to the mare once he'd gone. 'Men! Why do we like them?' Carmen asked as she put her arms around the mare's neck. 'I tell you now, if he was in *my* yard...' she looked into the velvet-brown eyes '...I'd fire him.'

She smiled at the very thought.

'No, I would never have hired him in the first place. Too damned good-looking, too cocksure,' she crooned, trying to calm Capricorn with her tone if not with her actual words as Dom was noisily brought out. 'It's fine,' Carmen soothed.

But then, as the yard quietened down once the stallion had been led out, so too did Carmen's indignity at being dressed down by Elias.

'Was I rude?' she asked Capricorn as she mucked her stable out.

After all, it was easy to get complacent around horses; he was simply looking out for the new stable hand, not realising just how expert she was.

And as for accusing her of being arrogant...?

Carmen knew very well that she was!

Should she apologise?

Only, that would mean talking to him.

Taking her lunch from her satchel, she headed over to the north field, where Domitian was running and letting off steam as Elias leant on the gate and watched.

'I apologise if I was rude,' Carmen mumbled as she came to stand beside him.

'Excuse me?'

You heard, Carmen wanted to say.

'I apologise,' she said more clearly. 'I appreciate that you were just looking out for me, although I *was* keeping one eye on Winnie…'

'Fair enough,' he conceded. 'Still, I'd suggest you keep both eyes—' He halted the lecture. 'Look, I'm not a fan of cell phones. Especially when Domitian is around.'

'Believe me, I wouldn't have my cell phone out if I was dealing with him.'

She smiled, and then took off her gloves and opened the lid on her lunch box, ignoring the fruit salad and pulling out a quesadilla filled with cheese and last night's chilli.

'I'm supposed to cook tonight,' Carmen said conversationally. Seeing him glance at her lunch, she held it out. 'Do you want half?'

'No.' He shook his head. 'No, thank you.'

'Where I come from, it's rude to refuse,' she insisted. But he ignored her, so she looked at Dom. 'He's showing off.'

Carmen smiled as she watched the black stallion pick up his legs and prance. Then, perhaps sensing a new audience, he started to canter around the field.

But her smile waned as she felt the discomfort between her and Elias. Perhaps she should take her lunch elsewhere. She had made her apology, after all, but just as she was about to depart, he spoke.

'What are you making?' he asked, and she felt a little light flare in her chest, because he had initiated conversation.

'Paella,' Carmen said. 'A family recipe.'

'Sounds good.'

'They're all very much looking forward to it…' Carmen sighed, trying not to feel daunted, but brightened up as she watched Dom. 'He's done dressage?'

'Yes,' Elias said, briefly turning from Domitian's showing off to take in Carmen's arms, resting on the rails and her face brown with dust and streaked with sweat.

Elias had *not* been eyeing her lunch. Instead, when she'd removed her gloves, he'd noticed her slender hands.

Carmen really was beautiful.

He had known it, of course, but had not properly allowed himself to acknowledge it until now. He was surprised to realise that a glimpse of her slender fingers had him wanting to see her toes...

Damn! The last thing he needed was to have the hots for the new stable hand.

The staff here lived and worked together, but Elias kept himself well away from all that.

LA was for work and recreation.

Malibu was his haven—where he relaxed, where he let his guard down...

Because even when it came to sex, his guard was never down.

As for relationships...?

There was no such thing.

He turned his attention back to Domitian, who had boldly made his way over. The stallion was heading straight for Carmen.

'Whoa!' Elias commanded.

To his credit, Domitian did as he was told, coming to an abrupt halt—albeit with a challenging stare. It was more than a stare. He flashed his teeth and flattened his ears.

Elias, used to it, calmly turned to Carmen, still keeping the stallion in his peripheral vision, but not offering a direct challenge that might cause confrontation. It was an obvious tactic, and he rolled his eyes at Carmen as they looked at each other, both deliberately ignoring Dom's challenge.

'I think he wants a treat,' Carmen said, knowing exactly why Dom had bounded towards her, given that she'd been bribing him with liquorice all week.

'Well, he's not getting one,' Elias said.

'Give him a strawberry,' Carmen suggested, knowing she had some in her lunch box.

'Not when he's staring me down.'

She felt guilty again, knowing exactly why Dom had come over, and told herself that that was why she blushed. 'He's still staring...'

'So we'll just keep ignoring him,' Elias replied. 'As you can tell, the lunatic really has taken over the asylum.'

Carmen laughed. 'At home we say the wolf is guarding the sheep.'

'Where *is* home?' he asked.

'Spain.'

'I had worked that much out, Carmen. Whereabouts in Spain?'

'The south.'

Carmen didn't want to elaborate and was deliberately evasive. Jerez was famous for its dancing Andalusian horses, as well as its festivals, and she didn't want a conversation that would lead them there or give him enough information that he would figure out who she was.

Because Carmen rather liked being here.

She liked who she was here.

Then she met his gaze and acknowledged that she *very* much liked being here.

'Finally!' Elias said, as Domitian snorted and took himself off.

They leant on the fence again, and Carmen ventured a little more about herself, though it was nothing she hadn't already told Blake.

'I've worked with dressage horses before. I could do some work with Dom,' Carmen offered. 'There was a two-year-old Criollo once, and I managed to—'

'Carmen, I hardly think—' He stopped, clearly checking his tone, which she could hear had veered towards derision. 'Criollo are easy-going.'

'Hmm...' she said. She didn't fully agree with him.

'What does *"hmm"* mean?'

'Had you not cut me off, I would have explained further...' she teased him.

It was just banter, she told herself. Because here she was free and could be anyone she wanted to be. She had no intention of revealing the true extent of her skills and training, but the secret knowledge of it gave her the confidence to toy with him.

'So, now you don't get to know.'

He gave a half-smile, clearly not believing a stable hand could really have anything of benefit to offer in this situation.

So she persisted. 'Have you ever considered—?'

'Carmen,' he cut in. 'We're working on it. And, while I can see you have no fear around horses, sometimes a little fear is a good thing.'

'I do have fear,' she corrected.

'Then you do a very good job of hiding it.' He shook his head. 'Look, I've solicited more opinions on Dom than I can count. He's already seeing an equine psychotherapist—'

'Both of you see the therapist together?' Carmen checked, with a mischievous edge to her tone.

'Yep,' he said, laughing. 'And, let me tell you, it's the closest to couple's therapy I'll ever get.'

Carmen laughed too.

'Look, Blake and I are both going to put more time in with him.' Elias let out a breath. 'Well, that's the plan. Depending on...you know...the LA stuff.'

She knew he was referring to his work outside of the polo yard. 'The grooms say you finance movies?'

'Not me personally.' He let out a low, slightly mirthless laugh. 'It's an investment firm. I mainly do the risk assessments.'

It was Elias holding back now. Holding back the fact that he'd far rather be *here* than *there*—how the board were demanding more, his father was demanding more. Not because the firm wasn't doing well, but because they were. And of course they wanted more, more, *more*...

He settled for: 'It's pretty full-on. Of course it's full-on here too, and unfortunately I can't be in two places at once.'

'There needs to be two of you.' Carmen smiled.

'There used to be.'

Even as her mind translated his words into Spanish she opened her mouth to respond. But for once she was grateful for that slight pause the translation allowed for, because it halted the light-hearted comment she'd been about to make and she recalled something Laura had said.

'You lost someone?'

'Joel—my twin.'

'I'm sorry.'

'You weren't to—' he started, but then took a quick breath. 'You didn't hear my speech at the awards night?'

'No.' She shook her head. 'I was busy getting myself fired.'

'Ah, yes.' He smiled, clearly recalling the small diversion she had caused.

'Well, I heard the bit when you spoke about grief,' Carmen admitted. 'How old was he when he died?'

'Thirty,' Elias said, and then added rather pointedly. 'We were talking on the phone when it happened. He was driving and I was— Well, I heard—'

Carmen swallowed, understanding a little better now why he'd been so cross earlier. 'I'm sorry,' she said. 'That must have been...' Her voice faded. 'I can't think of the right word.'

'I don't think there is one,' he said, 'in either of our languages.'

He turned his attention back to Dom, and although she rather guessed he'd prefer that she leave it there, she couldn't. 'Identical twins?'

'No,' he said, and breathed out a half-laugh that Carmen couldn't decipher. 'We weren't identical in any way...'

He didn't elaborate. But before she knew what he was doing, Elias had jumped the fence and was approaching the stallion, ready to do some work with him.

Playtime was over.

CHAPTER SEVEN

OCCASIONALLY THERE WAS an amnesty between them. Some nights, when they passed each other on the beach, he would nod to her; other nights he would be too far in the distance.

'Look at that,' she marvelled on one such night, more to herself than to Capricorn, as she watched Dom rear up while Elias leaned in and clung on to his back with his strong thighs.

They both looked magnificent, Carmen thought. Elias because he allowed the animal to be himself while remaining in complete control, and Domitian because he was simply a beautiful creature.

Some evenings Elias didn't acknowledge her at all.

'Don't mind him,' said John, who was riding Rocky at the time. He must have seen her face as Elias galloped past without even looking. 'He's like that with everyone. Well, not his fancy friends in the city…'

Carmen wanted to correct John, because that wasn't the man she had come to know, but then she thought of how he'd been when she'd first arrived. And then, as she thought of the awards night when she'd first met him, telling that blonde woman to go to hell and snapping at his date, she wanted to correct John again.

Elias *was* like that with *everyone*.

Though perhaps, at times, not with her…

* * *

The next night when it just Carmen and Capricorn on the beach Elias reined Dom into a walk as he approached them. He wore short boots that were as scruffy as her own for his rides on the beach, so it wasn't his casual attire that was different. There was just a more relaxed feeling in the air.

'*Hola,*' Carmen said, and now when she put up her hand to stroke Dom, Elias no longer warned her off.

She gently stroked the soft nose and the stallion nudged at her shorts.

'I had treats in there!' Carmen laughed.

'Not for him, I hope.'

'Of course not,' she lied. 'My boss won't let me,' she said with a wry smile.

She stroked Dom's ears and, although she spoke to the horse, it was clear for whom her words were intended.

'I'd love to work with you, Dom, if only your owner wasn't so determined to keep you all to himself.'

'Carmen, even *I* can't handle him some days! His previous owner was going to destroy him. And he threw your predecessor—'

'From everything I've heard, *I* would throw Martin.'

'Maybe…' Elias laughed and jumped down.

It was as though, on occasion, they called a truce, he thought. On certain evenings he found the opportunity to be on the receiving end of a dose of her opinionated conversation irresistible.

The fact was, she turned him on, just not in the usual way.

It wasn't simply about chemistry—though there was plenty of that. It was that she turned him on with her laugh, and the way she nudged him and pestered him to let her ride the stallion. It was the way they caught up on stable yard gossip—nothing indiscreet, just everyday chatter.

'I hear you made the most amazing paella,' Elias said now.

'I did!' Carmen smiled, hoping he couldn't see her burning cheeks.

It was the only time since she'd got to America that she'd cheated. Instead of foisting her lack of culinary skills on her hungry, hardworking housemates, she'd caved and arranged a secret delivery from a very swish restaurant.

'What are you making next week?' he asked.

'I haven't decided…'

He loved how she blushed as she lied, and laughed silently to himself at how the entire staff had seen the restaurant truck rumbling up the drive and the driver unloading not bags of ingredients but dishes of food.

She was a mystery—one that made him smile.

He enjoyed the view as she bent to pick up a piece of sea glass from the beach. It wasn't just the backs of her toned thighs that tightened his groin, but the pout on her lips as she examined it, the scrutiny in her eyes as she held up the piece of glass to the light before discarding it with a huff.

'Brown!' she scowled, and tossed it back.

'What's wrong with brown?'

'It's everywhere. I'm always looking out for orange.'

'Why orange?'

'Because in the olden days they didn't make many orange things.' Carmen shrugged. 'It's very rare. There's lots of brown sea glass, and I have a few turquoise pieces too, but no orange.'

'What about this one?' he asked a while later.

She was about to tell him that green was as common as brown, and that she had a hundred pieces like this, but suddenly she knew there could never be one as beautiful as this, because this one came from long fingers that had selected it just for her...

She saw that the hairs on his knuckles were gold from the sun, that his nails were neat, but the skin on his palms was strong and rough.

Carmen wore gloves for a reason.

She had to present herself as picture-perfect at family events.

But Elias...

She looked at his hands again and wanted so badly to touch them, to know how that tough skin felt against hers.

'It's beautiful,' she said, and took the glass from him, slipping it into her pocket.

She knew that her plan not to like him was fading as fast as the setting sun.

'Do you miss Spain?' he asked one night, having returned to the ranch following a long day of meetings in LA.

'Yes!'

She knew she sounded surprised, and saw him turn and look at her.

'Had you asked me a couple of weeks ago, I would have said no. But since working here, at the yard...'

She went misty-eyed as she thought of Presumir.

'How long are you in the US for?'

'Three months,' Carmen said. 'Well, I guess there are only a few weeks left now...'

Her voice faded away as it dawned on Carmen that she was going to miss being here too.

Miss moments like this...

'She's tired,' Carmen said, referring to Capricorn, whose pace had started to drop off. 'I should get her back.'

'Sure.'

But in her stable Capricorn refused to settle.

'Lie down for me, girl,' Carmen said to the mare.

But even when she got the pregnant mare to lie down, she was still unsettled—as though the second Carmen left she might stand up again.

'I used to be like that,' Carmen said, and she lay down with the tired mare.

She told her about the nanny who had raised her after her mother left.

'As soon as Paula tried to turn out the light I would sit up and ask her a question or ask for some water.'

She lay there, remembering, but was brought suddenly back to the present as the little foal within Capricorn moved. Carmen smiled, as the mare lay quietly, accepting the movement and completely unfazed.

'You're going to be a wonderful mother,' Carmen said, and Capricorn responded with a breathy *hmmph*. 'Better than mine, anyway.'

It was Carmen who hmmphed this time.

She could hear the yard quietening down as the soft light of evening fell. She took out her phone and saw that there was another message from Emily, which included some more photos of her little niece.

Josefa was eight months old now, but she had been born twelve weeks early, so was still tiny. She was catching up fast, though, and for the very first time Carmen saw herself in her niece. She was blonde, like Emily, but she had dark almond-shaped eyes and was starting to get fat cheeks...

Carmen loved little Josefa with all her heart, but this evening the sight of her niece made her want to cry. The little girl was so close to the age Carmen had been when her mother had walked out...

'How could you leave a little girl like that?' she asked a dozing Capricorn, who of course didn't reply.

How could her mother have just decided, when Carmen had been less than a year old, that she wanted no part in her life?

And then twenty-five years later decide to return?

She heard hooves then, and the sound of boots. She sat up, only realising then that she'd been crying.

'Maldito,' she cursed, and quickly wiped her eyes as she stood up, certain that Elias wouldn't appreciate finding her lying down with one of the horses—or ponies, or whatever they were called here.

'Carmen?' he said, frowning when he glanced in and saw that she was there.

'Capricorn took a while to settle,' Carmen said, letting herself out.

He looked at the straw in Carmen's hair and she knew he'd guessed she'd been lying down with the pregnant mare. He looked as if he was about to tell her off, but perhaps he saw how red her eyes were, and that her lashes were damp and decided she did not need scolding right now.

'She looks peaceful,' Elias said.

'Yes,' Carmen agreed.

She took a deep breath to calm herself, and it was at that very second that she fully encountered his scent. Cologne, she guessed, left over from his day spent in meetings in LA. She picked up little notes of citrus and wood—or was it wood smoke? The kind you encountered when you rode through the hills in winter? And there was another scent… one she had never really been aware of before…which she knew had to be the potent edge of masculinity, because it made her want to step closer and breathe deeper.

And then she recalled the chest and back and flat stomach she had seen that first morning…

'I'm just going to do a final check and then head to bed,' Carmen croaked. 'It's good to finally be tired.'

'Yeah,' he said.

'I mean...'

She opened her mouth to explain that her head was not tired—that it hadn't been for most of her life, and certainly not since her father died. That she meant *physically* tired, and that felt like a blessing.

'It doesn't matter...' She put up a hand, as if to say it was too hard to explain, but...

Elias nodded.

'Yep.'

He'd kill to be tired tonight.

Instead of hard for Carmen.

CHAPTER EIGHT

'You're sure about tomorrow?' Blake checked as Carmen headed out for her evening walk with Capricorn. 'I can get someone in…'

'No need.' Carmen shook her head. 'I wouldn't know how to…' She paused to recall one of the many new expressions she had learnt. 'How to "man the line". It all sounds very chaotic.'

'We wouldn't have you manning the line.' Blake grinned. 'There's always a lot of other stuff to do, though, and—'

'Well, I'm sure Laura's busy enough without training me on the job at a semi-final.'

'Fair enough,' Blake said. 'I'll see you bright and early tomorrow.'

'I'll be up long before it's bright,' Carmen said with a smile.

But as soon as she walked away she let her smile drop.

Elias hadn't been at the yard today, and she had missed seeing him far too much for comfort.

So, no, she did *not* want to be at the polo semi-final tomorrow and get caught up in this intriguing sport. Nor did she want to watch Elias compete…

Carmen attempted to switch off that thought but it wasn't as easy as turning off her smile. Her mind kept flickering towards it as she took Capricorn out a little deeper into the sea, pleased that the mare was really enjoying it.

'See?' Carmen said as she stood waist-deep in the ocean next to the gentle horse. 'It's nice for your legs and that big belly…'

Capricorn had certainly got a lot bigger in the past couple of weeks.

Today had been Carmen's first taste of a really hot Californian day, so it could well be the case, she told herself, that the weather was to blame for her pensive mood now. She wore denim shorts and a yellow bikini top, and for once was without her phone.

She was sick and tired of the pressure from her brothers to get the legal ball rolling over the house, as well as exhausted by calls from Maria, pleading her case.

'Carmen, I know was absent, I know that I hurt you, but I came back. I was there for your father and I'm trying to be here for you now. You're the one who's left…you're the one in America…'

'Nice?' she said to Capricorn, scooping water over her back.

Yet even with Capricorn's antics Carmen struggled to smile.

It wasn't just her family issues niggling at her…

She looked at her arms and, though they were still slender, saw that her biceps were certainly coming on. Taking sets of four or five horses out for hours each morning and wrestling their different temperaments along with their reins was good for her.

'Maybe I *could* man the line,' Carmen grumbled, suddenly upset with herself for refusing Blake's offer, knowing it had confused him, and no doubt the other grooms too…

Why *wouldn't* she want to go and watch the game they'd spent hours of every day preparing the horses for?

But, no, she didn't want to be dripping sweat and covered in horse hair and worse while all those elegant beauties were cool in the shade or under a gorgeous hat, sipping champagne...

Would Wanda be there? Or would it be one of his in-betweens?

Carmen was jealous, and she knew it. Though she firmly told herself it wasn't because she *liked* Elias. Of course it wasn't *that*, she scoffed. She was jealous of his confidence, his inhibition. She wished she could date casually, like he did...

'Why shouldn't I?' Carmen said aloud, leaving Capricorn to kick her hooves in the shallows while she took a seat on the beach.

She picked at the coral varnish on her toenails, wishing she'd brought her phone so she could try this internet dating that Laura kept telling her about...

But wasn't Laura sleeping with John?

And she was fifty years old!

Not that age had ever stopped her parents. They'd been having sex when Papá had died—as Maria loved to reveal to anyone who stood still long enough to breathe in her presence.

Carmen had sworn off men and relationships a long time ago, and yet her twenty-six-year-old body seemed to have decided otherwise...

What is this sex thing we've been missing out on? it enquired as she lay in bed at night. *Why do you have to take it all so seriously?* it demanded, as she woke to the sound of Laura and John...

And now, with her ocean-soaked shorts riding up uncomfortably as she sat on the beach, those night-time thoughts were creeping in to her days too.

She turned when she heard Dom's now familiar gait, and was surprised by the unexpected sight of Elias on the eve of the semi-final.

'Hey,' he said, having pulled Dom to a halt.

'Hola,' Carmen said, annoyed at how her heart leapt. 'She's cooling off,' Carmen said, nodding towards Capricorn.

'I might let him go in too,' Elias said.

Dom needed no encouragement or goading. As soon as he was unsaddled he went straight in, and Carmen laughed at the stallion's obvious delight as he rolled onto his back and scissored his front legs.

With Dom safely loose in the water, Elias tried not to notice Carmen's bare stomach, or that her nipples were pebbled beneath the wet bikini top. He took off his scruffy boots and joined her in sitting on the shoreline, pretending to be engrossed in the horses' antics, while noting that even her feet were sexy.

'How's the real job?' Carmen asked.

'I signed off on a big project today,' he said, nodding.

'You did your risk assessments?'

'This one's a pretty safe bet.'

'Is there such a thing in movies?'

'Yep,' he said, nodding again.

That producer had been right; the script was a guaranteed winner.

'Well, so long as the leading actor doesn't fall off the wagon…'

He sighed and closed his eyes, as if to shut out the long and tedious past couple of weeks.

Carmen's arrival had been something of a saving grace…

'Are you looking forward to tomorrow?' she asked.

'Not really,' Elias replied, his eyes still closed. He was surprised by his own honesty.

'You'll miss him…?'

'Yep.' He didn't pretend not to understand her meaning. 'Joel would rock up in the morning with these disgusting vitamin juice drinks…'

'I made them for a while,' Carmen said with a snort. 'When I first came to the States I got a job in a juice bar. They're disgusting.'

'I used to feed mine to Homer.'

'Who's Homer?'

'My horse before Capricorn,' he said, and then frowned, trying to fathom why he felt that she ought to already know that. Had she really only been here for a couple of weeks? 'My parents always come for a final.'

'Will they be there tomorrow?'

'They'll be there,' he said. 'The first time they'll have been to a match since—' No, he was definitely not looking forward to tomorrow. 'You're not coming?'

'Someone has to stay back.'

'Blake said he offered to get in a casual.'

'I told him there was no need for that. I'm more than happy to stay.'

Elias leant back on his forearms and turned his head to look at her, but it was as if Carmen refused to look back at him. 'You don't want to see what all the fuss is about?' he asked.

'Not really.' Carmen shrugged.

Elias wasn't sure if it was her shrug that irked him, or his own disappointment that she wouldn't be there tomorrow to watch him play. 'You're really not interested in watching a polo match?'

'Not particularly,' Carmen stated, staring out at the rolling waves and wondering why, on a hot Malibu night, she could be so cold. She was unsure too as to why her defences were suddenly up. 'Anyway, I doubt I'd get to see much. It sounds like the grooms are kept rather busy.'

They loved it, though, Carmen knew, but there was something gnawing at her that kept her from relaxing.

She turned and gave him a tight smile. 'What happens if you win tomorrow?'

'We make the grand final. It's being held the following week.'

'I know that. I mean what happens after the match?'

'Oh.' He thought for a moment. 'There's an after-party at Ramone's—though I suspect it'll be our opponents celebrating.'

'Ramone's?' Carmen frowned. 'Isn't that quite a formal venue? I thought Laura said everyone usually just headed to a bar.'

'The grooms do their own thing. Still, there's a grand ball after the final, for all the teams that took part. The grooms go too.'

Carmen pulled a face. 'Well, if you make it, I'll be putting up my hand to stay back for the final too. I don't exactly have a ballgown stashed in my backpack. Anyway, I hate formal functions,' she told him. 'What about you?'

'I don't mind them. It's part of the tournament.'

'You looked pretty miserable the other week.' She glanced over. 'Both you *and* your partner...'

He stared ahead in silence and Carmen knew she'd crossed a line few would dare.

'I wouldn't call her that.'

'What, then?'

He didn't answer for a very long time. In fact, when he spoke he didn't answer at all. 'You ask a lot of questions.'

'I'm just making conversation.'

But Carmen knew then what was really churning her insides.

'Wanda accompanies me to formal functions and such.'

Carmen pursed her lips.

Elias never usually explained himself, yet somehow he felt it necessary. 'She knows that I don't want to be tied to any other person.'

'That sounds very definite.'

'Because I *am* very definite.' He made it a warning.

'Why?' Carmen turned to him. 'Don't you believe in romance or love?'

'It's not for me.'

'Why?'

'Isn't that what three-year-olds do?' He tried to deflect her. 'Ask why? Why? Why?'

'Oh, I was a lot younger than three when I started asking *por qué*?' Carmen told him. 'And I've never stopped.'

He smiled at her persistence. 'I'd just prefer not to get that close to anyone.'

'Have you ever been?'

'Not really…' He pondered her question. 'I was seeing someone when Joel died, though we broke up soon after.'

'Por qué?' Carmen asked.

He gave a reluctant laugh. 'When we were first going out I was living the LA life—I would came here at weekends, but it was more of a hobby. Then, after Joel died, I spent more and more time here… At the end of the day, I didn't want to involve anyone else in how I was feeling. And I still don't.'

It was another warning.

'So, is Wanda a paid escort?'

'Carmen!'

'Excuse me!' She gave him a small, apologetic smile. 'My English is terrible sometimes. I know that I can come across as too direct.'

His eyes narrowed, and she saw a reluctant smile on his lips, even though he clearly knew she was lying. 'Your English is excellent, Carmen.'

'Thank you.'

'And no, I don't pay for company. I have to go to these events and Wanda likes to network, so it benefits us both.'

'So, do you sleep together?'

'I'm not discussing that.'

They sat in silence for a very long time.

It was Elias who spoke first. 'Do you?'

'Do I what?'

'Believe in love and romance.'

Carmen gave a scoffing laugh. 'No.' She shook her head. 'I've given up on dating.'

She scuffed the sand with her heel and then, sitting up, pulled up her knees and rested her head on them, turning to look over at him.

'My father desperately wanted to walk me down the aisle. He saw every man I dated as a future husband.'

'What about you?'

'I wanted to make my father happy.'

'Wanted?'

Carmen nodded. 'He died last year.'

'I'm sorry.'

'Please don't...'

She put up a hand to halt his sympathies. It still felt too new, too raw, to talk about. But it wasn't just words he was offering, because his hand gently rested on her bare shoulder.

Usually Carmen pulled away from physical contact, but there was comfort in his hand, and it steadied her enough to dwell on the moment. Elias was the first person she'd told about her father who had never met him. It felt like some bizarre milestone...one she didn't want to unpick.

Then he removed his hand, but that rare feeling of comfort remained.

A lovely wave came and kissed her toes and Carmen smiled, saying, 'The tide is turning.'

She closed her eyes, missing his hand on her shoulder, knowing his eyes roamed her body, feeling her spine tingling as if he'd run a light finger down it.

'My father had terrible taste. He adored the last boyfriend I had, but...'

'Did you?'

'We weren't together for long, but I actually thought he was a nice guy for once.'

Why she was sharing her shame, Carmen didn't know. Well, she wouldn't tell him about the money, because she didn't want to reveal her background, or how well-known she was back in Spain. The only alternative was to reveal the part of her life that had stung the most.

'I overheard him telling his friend that I smelt of the stables and that he had to— Well, anyway, some other not nice things too.'

Telling Elias, watching his reaction, she felt her embarrassment over the long ago incident evaporate. *Poof!* Gone.

Because he just looked at her.

And *how* he looked...

Carmen had never been looked at like that before. It was as if he wanted to lean over and inhale her neck, or lift her arm and kiss the tender inside and say, *I beg to differ...*

There was nothing she could pinpoint, no apparent change in his demeanour, but he looked, and she smouldered beneath his gaze. She saw the dark ring around his chocolate irises and felt something heavy in the air between them. She felt the weight of her own lips, and as the object of his studied attention she felt…

Wanted.

She felt kissed.

For a moment, just a second—it didn't even equate to time—Carmen felt wanted in a way she'd never known before. So wanted that the most natural thing to do was surely to move her face towards his…

She'd never met such power. The ocean was a mere puddle compared to the absolute pull that shot through her, and it made her want to lean in and know his kiss for real.

It took everything she had to resist, to remind herself that she had no idea what she was doing…

'I should get going…' she croaked.

'Of course,' Elias said calmly as Carmen stood up.

She had known she had a crush on him. Was attracted to him. With his looks and charm it was perhaps a matter of course. Yet what she had felt just now had been far from a matter of course. To kiss him would have felt natural.

Normal.

Necessary.

Her cheeks were suddenly stinging, her legs felt unsteady and her voice quivered as she called Capricorn in from the water.

'Enjoy your night,' she said to Elias.

'And you.'

Capricorn settled easily, thank goodness, because Carmen didn't want to be around when Elias returned. Or rather, she desperately *did* want to be around when Elias returned.

Because she wanted to revisit that moment and claim the kiss she felt she had denied by walking away.

She made her way to the lodge, thankful that everybody else was either out or already in bed.

Using her cell phone to light the way, she climbed the creaking steps. In her attic room she peeled off her damp shorts and bikini top and hung them over a chair, then pulled on a T-shirt and climbed into bed.

'I don't like you, Elias,' Carmen said aloud, as she slid into the dip in the middle of the lumpy mattress, her words a vain attempt to remind herself of her determination not to let anyone in.

She lay there, her body prickling from its first real exposure to the Californian sun. She sat up and took off her T-shirt to relieve her skin…

Only that didn't help. And Carmen knew it wasn't the sun that had turned her body to fire.

And it was there, lying naked in the soft darkness of the night, that it dawned on Carmen that she was finally finding herself…

With Elias, it felt as if she was discovering the sensual side of herself.

Carmen hadn't even been aware that she could feel like that…like this… She had told herself that Elias would never deign even to look at a stable hand…

Yet he had.

That someone as worldly and sexy as Elias might actually want her, purely for herself, felt liberating. That she, Carmen, could be caressed with his eyes when he knew nothing about her family, her money, her inheritance…

She rolled onto her stomach and pressed her forehead into her arm, willing sleep to come.

She wanted to know his kiss…

More than his kiss.

Carmen had come to America to discover herself, to find out what kind of person she was without the Romero name opening doors for her. And now that she was actually starting to... Well, it turned out that she *was* capable of attraction and lust and all the things that had eluded her until now.

Next time he looked at her like that...

She lay there, on fire, certain of one thing: there absolutely would be a next time.

And when that next time came, Carmen wanted more than a kiss...

CHAPTER NINE

Elias didn't feel as if it was semi-final day.

'No green juice for you,' he said to Homer as he gave the Misfits their treats and then headed over to the yard.

And no parents dropping by, as they always had when he and Joel had played for the old team.

'*Hola!*' Carmen was tying Winnie's tail as if she'd done it a thousand times. 'She's on fire this morning. She could make it to Vegas and back.'

'Good to know!'

'Vegas?' Laura looked up from the horse's leg she was strapping. 'You so have to go there, Carmen.'

'Oh, I'm going to,' Carmen said assuredly.

'I saw the best psychic there.'

Elias had rolled his eyes, because Laura was clearly about to start a monologue on her favourite pastime, when Carmen chimed in, 'Well, I want to see a show and play the tables.'

Why, Elias pondered, when he had a million things to do, was he standing here listening to his head groom and his junior stable hand chatter on? And, more to the point, why was he joining in?

'Red or black?' he asked.

'Red,' Carmen said. 'Every time.'

'Do you gamble?' he asked.

'Never.' She shook her head. 'But if I did, it would be—' Her voice halted as Blake called out for him. 'Blake's calling.'

'Yep,' he said, nodding, and tore his focus away from Carmen.

He reluctantly got back to his busy day as his yard manager made his way over.

'Laura, the truck's ready. Elias, Wanda's calling; she can't get you on your cell phone.'

'Sure.'

Carmen found she was biting her lip as she finished off Winnie's tail. She kept telling herself it didn't matter as she helped load the horses into a huge, luxurious horse truck and the rest of the team went off to get changed.

Elias had changed too, and came out of his office in fresh attire and long, gleaming black boots. And Blake was looking very smart.

'It's a shame you're missing it,' he said as he went to do a final check on the animals before the truck headed off with its precious cargo.

Oh, no, it wasn't, Carmen thought.

It hurt her that Wanda would be there.

Bitterly.

More than that, it angered her.

Oh, she hadn't expected flowers and romance from a playboy, but common decency would do! She knew she hadn't imagined that moment on the beach last night.

Not that she would let on.

Carmen pushed out a smile for Blake. 'Good luck!'

And she said the same to each member of the team as they piled into the coach that would take them to the venue.

'Why aren't you coming?' John asked.

'Because…' Carmen took a breath, her anger building.

She wished everyone would simply go, so she could run into a field and scream…

'If we win, we'll let you know where the party is!' Laura called.

'I hate parties.'

Carmen waved them off in the coach, then turned and found herself face to face with Elias's scent and his chest.

'Shouldn't you already be gone?' she asked.

'On my way…'

He looked stunning…elegant and polished. He stood there, waiting for her to speak, and she knew damn well what he expected. After all, she'd spent the last fifteen minutes wishing everyone else luck, and now she stood before the owner of the team.

But Carmen was too angry to play nice. 'Yes?' she said, rather directly. 'Is there something you need?'

'Nothing.' He went to go but then clearly changed his mind. 'Wishing someone good luck is generally considered polite…'

'You don't need luck, Elias.' She took a tense breath. She knew he was probably as superstitious before an event as she was, and she wouldn't want to feel responsible for him losing. *'Buena suerte,'* Carmen snapped. 'I wish you luck in Spanish.'

'Hey!' Elias frowned. 'What *is* your problem?'

'No problem,' she said, all too aware that if she blew her temper now, it would be the fourth job she'd lost…

Only, this had nothing to do with work.

Nothing.

Her eyes met his and she could feel her chest rising and falling, hear her own breath in her chest. Suddenly, she couldn't stop herself.

'How dare you look at me as you did last night and then

expect me not to be angry when I hear your date waits for you today!'

'What the hell...?'

'You heard me,' Carmen said. 'You kissed me last night with your eyes—you know damn well that you did.'

'What does that even *mean*?'

'You know exactly what it means—and you know too that we could have taken it all the way to bed!' She was furious. 'You're damn lucky I won't be at the match today. Because if I'd seen her there I'd have slapped your cheek!'

'And that,' Elias snapped, 'is exactly why I don't do relationships! We haven't even kissed and you expect me to answer to you?' He turned on one booted heel. 'You're unreal,' he called out as he walked off.

'I'm right!' she called out. 'And you know it.'

Illogical?

Maybe.

Over the top?

Carmen did not care.

She had standards, and she was setting them for herself, here in this beautiful land where she was finding herself. Her heart was shattered, yet bit by bit she felt as if it was beginning to beat again...as if a brave new heart was blossoming...

'Your master is an arrogant bastard,' she told Dom as she fed him a treat before heading over to Capricorn. 'I hate men,' she told the mare, who nudged her to go for a walk. 'Come on, then,' she said.

But walking Capricorn on the beach did little to cool her temper. Worse, though, embarrassment was starting to emerge. Carmen knew that she'd revealed to Elias how attracted she was to him, and as well as that she knew she could be demanding.

But he'd probably laughed the whole episode off by the

time he'd got to his vehicle, no doubt used to the hired help having a crush on him…

Her phone rang.

'What?' she snapped as she answered Alejandro's call.

'Just reminding you it's Emily birthday…'

'I know. I've sent her a present.'

'No,' Alejandro said. 'You messaged my assistant and asked her to get something.'

'What do you want from me, Alejandro? Am I to call and sing "Happy Birthday"?'

'She'd love it if you did. You can be so damned selfish, Carmen. Emily doesn't have any family.'

'And if you break up? Am I still to ring and wish her Happy Birthday next year?'

'Why do you always have to assume the worst?'

Because it was all she knew.

Carmen's day didn't get better after that, and the news that the team had won the match did little to improve her mood.

For all the excited chatter that came with the win, there were still tired horses to be unloaded and cared for.

'You should have seen them!' Laura was beaming. 'They won every chukka. Elias smashed it.'

'Fantastic!' Carmen beamed back.

'Elias said we can have the coach for the night, so we can party anywhere we like…'

John, like Carmen, was perhaps a little tired of hearing Laura rave about their super-talented and generous boss, because he snapped, 'We get the coach, and he's getting suited up for the after-party at Ramone's.'

'We're in the final!' Laura just laughed at his grumpy mood. 'Win or lose, next week we're going to a proper ball.'

'Lucky us,' John muttered.

As they all headed off to get changed, Carmen pushed out a smile as she once again declined Blake's kind offer to get someone in so she could join in with the celebrations.

'No need. I want to go to Santa Monica tomorrow, and I don't want to have a hangover on my day off.'

'Fair enough.'

She wasn't just cross with Elias, Carmen realised as her colleagues left, all showered and scented and ready to party... She was fed up with being seen in either dirty jodhpurs or scruffy shorts. She'd always loathed dressing up, but tonight Carmen found that she missed it—and that made her even more annoyed. She was tired of being a grubby stable hand and embarrassed at the thought of facing Elias again, having practically accused him of cheating on her after a mere look.

Carmen opened the fridge and ate a leg of chicken, then headed up the stairs to the attic and looked out towards the ranch, wondering if he was in there, celebrating with Wanda...

Of course he was, Carmen decided.

So what if he'd told her she accompanied him to formal functions but they weren't in a relationship? He hadn't denied that they were sleeping together, had he?

Or was she a media and family-friendly front to hide his appalling reputation?

Alejandro had had Mariana for events like that, and they certainly had been sleeping together. Sebastián hadn't even bothered with a regular date for appearances' sake; he'd been an unashamed playboy where women were concerned.

Her brothers' past behaviour was part of the reason why Carmen didn't want to get close to Emily or Anna. They might *appear* different now, but who was to say that they would stay faithful to their wives?

She stomped to the shower, peeling off her filthy, smelly clothes. Of course there was no hot water left, after the whole team had showered and gone out, and a cold shower did nothing to cool her temper down.

Pulling on a denim skirt and vest top, she lay on the saggy bed and tried to take deep, calming breaths. She picked up her phone, put a smile on her face and made the necessary call.

'*Cumpleaños feliz...*' she sang, and Emily laughed. She knew Alejandro would get the joke, and laugh too, because singing was so unlike Carmen. '*Cumpleaños feliz...*' she sang again, but then felt herself choking up.

And now Emily was crying too.

'Thank you,' she tearfully said. 'It's so lovely to hear from you. How is it there?'

'Oh, you know...' Carmen shrugged, but of course Emily didn't know. How could she? 'Emily, how did you—?' She stopped herself from asking, how shy, sweet Emily had dared risk her heart in the hands of a playboy and instead asked, 'How are you celebrating?'

'Didn't Alejandro tell you?' Emily said. 'We're in London!'

'Oh? When did you get there?'

'I didn't know anything about it. It was a surprise this morning. We're spending the day here, and tomorrow we're going to show Josefa where I grew up, and see Anna's parents.'

To Carmen's wounded, abandoned heart, Emily's words sounded like a threat. Her throat tightened. What if her brothers moved to England?

What was to stop two best friends deciding they both missed home?

There was no point getting close to anyone. Not when they would only leave her in the end.

'Well, I won't keep you…it sounds incredible.'

'Carmen?' Emily said hurriedly before Carmen could hang up. 'What are you doing? Do you ever get time off?'

'Not much,' Carmen said. 'In fact, I have to go and check on the horses for the night. Have a great trip.'

'Thank you for the perfume.'

'You're welcome. *Ciao!*'

The horses were all tired; even Capricorn was snoring. The only exception was Domitian, and she stood admiring possibly the most magnificent horse she had ever seen.

'Apart from Presumir!' she warned him, feeling his warm breath on the backs of her hands. 'I think I'll have to leave,' she told him. 'I made a fool of myself today.' She took a breath. 'So I'm never going to get to ride you.'

But why be sensible now?

She'd already made a mess of this day.

So she slipped into his stable…

'Come on,' she said, putting a soft bridle on him. 'Let's see what you can do.'

Carmen led him out to the old riding school arena, walking as casually as if she were taking Capricorn to the beach, but her heart was pounding.

There was little that was more unnerving than this— walking into an empty arena with a horse she knew could turn on her at any given second.

She turned on the lights and walked him to the centre of the arena. She held out her hand with a treat and spoke to him for a few moments, telling him what she meant to do. But then came the terrifying part.

Carmen turned her back on the stallion and walked away from him, eventually coming to a stop and standing motionless. It was a move meant to show Domitian that she had no fear, and that she expected him to respect her.

Domitian had to know he had her trust.

She could hear the blood whooshing in her ears as she stared at a knot in the wood of the gate, and then she swallowed as she felt Domitian's attention on her. He might attack, or kick. He might drag her around the arena, or slam her straight into the gate and crush her...

All this Carmen knew well, and yet this was what she did for a living...these were the animals she loved.

And here was her reward: the nudge of his nose in her back and his magnificent head coming down over her shoulder.

'Hola, caballo,' she crooned, and there were tears in her eyes as she turned and buried her face in his neck. 'Are you going to be good for me?

He was better than good.

Domitian was stunning.

She worked with him for a full hour, lightly instructing him with a stick, or a click of her tongue, loving how receptive he was.

'Are we really going to do this?' she asked, as he came over once more.

Without thinking twice, she gripped his mane and mounted him—no saddle, and certainly no stirrups. She was just trying him out, moving with him.

'Clever boy,' she said.

And he was such an incredible horse that she took him through a few basic movements.

And then some more.

When she did some flyover changes, it felt as if she was asking a high school student to spell *cat*. There was nothing this horse could not do.

Let's see...

She gave him an instruction and his hindquarters lowered.

'You complete star!' Carmen said, patting his neck. 'You could dance if I had time to train you.'

Gosh, he really was perfection, Carmen thought, and decided to try a levade—a move where the hindquarters were lowered fully and the front legs were lifted.

She held on to his mane and gave the signal. And she felt the absolute beauty as Dom moved and then brought his front legs up…

What the hell…?

Elias didn't even know if he'd said it out loud, but as he watched Dom rear up his impulse was to dash forward. And yet he knew it was imperative that he stay calm, so as not to spook the stallion.

Elias had felt pure terror once—the night Joel had died. Tonight, he felt it again.

Seeing that Dom was missing from his stable, and the lights were on in the old riding school arena, at worst he'd thought he might be about to catch Carmen doing some ground work with the bad-tempered beast. But not…*this*.

It was then that he realised he hadn't spoken out loud, for horse and rider hadn't noticed him, and he stood in silent awe, watching true poetry in motion.

He'd known Dom was stunning and had great potential, but it was the sight of Carmen that had reduced him to silent awe.

She was perfection…barely moving as the horse moved, an utter master as she brought him up again, onto his hindquarters, and then cantered around the arena a couple of times.

Even her long black hair barely rippled, and her brown legs were relaxed. She gracefully brought him to a halt and then did the manoeuvre again.

Elias wasn't sure if it was Dom or Carmen who saw him

first, but there was a slight wobble and a less than perfect landing as the horse lowered himself down.

'Good boy,' Carmen said, stroking his mane, and then added 'I think we've been busted.'

'Carmen...' he said, keeping his voice even with great difficulty. Even though his heart was still thumping in terror, he refused to be provoked, knowing that anything could unsettle Domitian. 'Get off him. *Now!*'

'I don't want to,' she said.

'Get. Off. Him.'

'We're fine.'

'Oh, I'm not asking,' he warned, and finally she met his eyes.

No, Elias was not asking; he was ordering her to get down.

He watched her dismount, as lightly as a cat jumping from a table, and then she calmly took some liquorice from her pocket and fed Domitian a treat.

'I'm taking him in,' Elias told her.

'I can manage,' she responded tartly. She looked at him again. 'Shouldn't you be at your after-party?'

'Do I look as if I've been at a party? Or going to one?'

Her eyes took in his attire, and he knew she must see that he was still in his match gear, but it didn't change her stance.

'I told you. I know what I'm doing.'

He said nothing. Just took a very pleased with himself and surprisingly well-behaved two-thousand-pound stallion back to his stable and bolted him in.

'Now he needs another treat,' Carmen said, and had the audacity to reach into the pocket of her skirt and take out some more liquorice.

'Is that what you've been bribing him with?' Elias snapped, and took the damned treat from her.

He patted and stroked the horse then, pretending that everything was completely fine, so as not to confuse the horse.

'Good boy,' he said nicely. 'Well done for not killing Carmen. Good Dom.'

Then he turned with eyes blazing.

'My office—now!'

He practically marched her there, and when she stepped into his office for the first time she saw not the gleaming desk, nor the leather chairs and sofa, only the blaze of his eyes.

'Clearly,' he said, 'you have no idea what you're doing!'

Carmen blinked. Elias was white-faced—she assumed it was with anger.

'You could have been killed!' he shouted. 'I swear to God, Carmen, if you've been taking him out alone, with no one around…'

He was livid, she could see that, and trying to contain it.

'You had no business taking him out without permission!'

'Would you have agreed if I'd asked?'

'We both know the answer to that,' he snapped. 'Can you imagine how it would have felt for Laura or Blake to find you unconscious on the floor? Or dead?'

He sucked in a tense, shuddering breath and closed his eyes for a moment, as if envisaging just that.

'Damn it, Carmen!'

There was only the sound of his heavy breathing in the silence that followed these words.

'Where do you think you're going?' he demanded as Carmen turned to leave.

'The animals are all settled,' she called over her shoulder. 'I'm now officially on my day off. You can get back to your date.'

'Date? What date? What the hell do you think I'm doing here?'

'I've no idea.'

'I came to say...' He took a breath. 'I came to say that you're wrong.'

She knew exactly what he was referring to. How could she not? It was all she had thought about all day long.

'No, no, no...' She shook her head. 'Listen to me, you arrogant man. I don't expect flowers, and I don't give a damn about your past, or what you do after I'm gone, but don't make out with your eyes and then go off with your date—'

'On that point you are correct,' he said. 'And that is why I called Wanda last night and told her...'

'Told her what?'

'That our arrangement is over.'

'So why did she call you today?'

'Because I promised her an introduction to a producer she's been trying to impress!'

And then, just like that, he did what they both knew was inevitable—what she had ached for last night. He kissed her fiercely, his mouth so full of demand that had he not held her so tightly she would have toppled over.

His jaw was rough and his tongue was probing—but then he suddenly pulled back, conflicted. 'We can't do this.'

'Why not?' she asked.

He stared down at her.

'You *know* why! Carmen, I don't want to mess things up here.'

She could see he was struggling to explain.

'I don't do relationships...' he said.

'I already know that.' She stared back at him. 'And I told you last night that I don't either.'

His mouth came down on hers again, and the kiss felt like an elixir, like nectar, and she kissed him back as if she knew how…because with Elias she did.

The skin of his neck was warm, and she coiled her slender arms around it and whimpered in relief as his hands slid beneath her T-shirt to her breasts.

'Oh…' she moaned as he freed her from her bra. 'Please…'

She straightened her arms above her head as he slid off her T-shirt and then greedily tugged at his, unable to wait a moment longer to feel his naked chest on her skin.

When it finally happened, it was sublime.

Bare skin…pressing, touching, sliding…but then he pulled his mouth away.

'Don't stop!' she panted, stunned that she could so readily want this. It was as if he had found the lost key to her defences, and she was terrified to lose the moment. There was more than a kiss required to soothe this burning.

'I want this…'

He crushed her lips with his mouth then, and she felt all his power. She liked it that he hadn't made promises that he would never keep—Carmen had had a lifetime of that. And she liked it that he did not want to invade her world.

'I want you…now…'

Now.

Her loneliness was hushed. Not just the ache for home, but the dark pit of emptiness was gone too, as if she'd come alive under his mouth and the grip of his hands.

He kissed her as he lowered her down onto the couch and she wrapped her legs around his waist. Deep, hungry kisses that made her feel both soothed and desperate. The best kisses possible because their faces were level.

His impatient hands lifted her skirt, so that it bunched around her hips.

If this was what she had been scared of, what she had avoided, then she did not know why. Because this was incredible.

She was the one driving this forward as she unhooked his jodhpurs. It had been on the cards, she realised, since the moment she had arrived in his pristine yard, and now all order and control was gone.

Elias had spent half a decade holding himself in check, never allowing himself to sink into the moment, or lose himself to pure pleasure. From every angle and in every way he exerted control. But now he felt it slipping away...

His office, his order—all was forgotten as they explored each other's mouths and bodies. He felt her hand gripping him, stroking him, too tentative and delicate a touch when his body was on fire.

He slid his hand into her knickers and felt that she was ready, so wet and ready, and he heard her throaty gasps as he encircled his base.

'Please...'

He could wait no longer. He pulled her knickers aside and eased himself into position—then thrust in with all the passion she demanded.

He was shocked at what could only be the tearing of virgin flesh...

Carmen had expected it to hurt, and it did, but it was also delicious—as if every star in the sky was spinning.

But she was hauled back down to earth by the question in his voice.

'Carmen?'

She opened her eyes and locked her gaze with his for

a moment. He seemed…angry. But she had no breath in her to respond to anything other than the feel of him inside her as she tried to acclimatise to this new sensation.

'Elias…' she begged as he pulled back, desperate to hold him inside her still.

She did not want him to stop, and he clearly got the message, because now he pushed in deeper, and it felt as if he were prising open the black sky.

'*Dios…*' she said, because the sensation was exquisite.

She buried her face in his shoulder as he pushed again, all the way in this time, and then out, and then in again, each measured, slow thrust stretching her, taking her deeper than she had ever thought possible, to new experiences and new places she had waited so long to explore.

Slowly, she wanted to say. But she had forgotten not just the English word but the Spanish word too. She couldn't speak. So instead she met his thrusts…moving with him, joining him.

It was like pushing off from a cliff-edge, diving into the freedom he gave.

'Elias…' She cried out his name as she shuddered inside, sensation sparking every cell in her body.

He took her to oblivion, and his groan as he came inside her was met by her startled shout of pleasure as she climaxed. The strength of her first orgasm, the pulses of pleasure, was so deep and unexpected that all she could do was collapse into it.

Elias lifted his head. 'Carmen, I…'

She did not want it to be over—not least because she knew he would have questions—so for now they both just sucked in air, eyeing each other and panting.

He pulled out and looked down at the blood, and then back at her.

'I think I must be getting my period…'

'Don't lie!' he warned as he tucked himself back in to his boxers. 'Not about this.'

'Elias…' She was trying to get her breath. 'Please don't make a big deal of it.'

'Don't even try to tell me I'm making a big deal of it.' He ran a hand through his shock of dark hair. 'If I had known you were a virgin—'

'What? You wouldn't have taken me, here in your office?' She laughed in his face. 'You'd have been all tender and—'

'I wouldn't have had sex with you in the first place.'

'Worried my heart can't take it?'

'Something like that.' He nodded.

'We both enjoyed it, Elias. That's all. Don't worry—I'm not going to fall in love with you.'

'Carmen, for goodness' sake!'

'No!' She stared angrily at him. 'I wanted you and you wanted me—and that's it. The end. You're the one who is complicating things.'

She got up and pulled on her top, heading for the door.

'We are going to talk,' he told her.

'About what?'

She was stunned—not at his reaction, but at the power of what had taken place. Intimacy was a huge issue for her, and she had never been so overtaken by desire, so utterly lost in the sensations of her body, wanting…

And Carmen did not want to explain it to him.

'I don't want commitment or promises. I never have. So don't worry about things changing, Elias.' She shook her head. 'I wanted sex, and so did you.'

'Don't walk away.'

'Go to your party,' Carmen replied.

'Don't be ridiculous.'

'What?' she said. 'Are we really going to sit down and talk now?'

It was the last thing she wanted. She didn't want to spoil the memory of what they had shared by putting it into words. She needed time and space to process it on her own first.

'I said I don't want to talk about it, Elias.'

Carmen wrenched open the office door and marched back to her attic room in the lodge. Even as she undressed and showered she could not quite believe the woman he'd made her tonight. She ran her hands over her skin under the spray of water and wondered at what she had just experienced.

And as she crawled into the most uncomfortable bed she'd ever slept in, she still couldn't understand her own lack of inhibition, the depth of her own desire.

Some things didn't need to be put into words...they could just *be*.

CHAPTER TEN

It WAS HER one day off in a fortnight and Carmen was in agony.

'That bastard!' she said, because it stung her to wee. 'What has he given me? *This* is why men cannot be trusted!'

Carmen feared the worst—because everything she was feeling right now was a first for her.

The lodge wasn't empty this morning, of course. John was there, eating from a bag of pretzels, and Carmen could barely manage a polite good morning, let alone ask about last night.

Not even picking out all the marshmallows from the box of cereal cheered her up.

'Any plans for today?' John asked.

'I'm going to Santa Monica.'

'There's a bus at ten.'

'Thanks.'

It was hell being poor—or pretending to be poor—Carmen thought as she stood waiting for a bus along with several others.

She was in agony. She was sore and swollen down below. And now she could ruefully admit to herself that she understood where Elias's anger had come from last night. After all, it had all been very fast and hard. She was paying for it now.

She winced again, and was tempted to cheat on her promise to herself not to spend more than she made. Unable to bear the wait for the bus any longer, she took out her phone, and she was just about to order a cab when a familiar silver car slid to a halt beside her.

Elias.

The window slid down.

'What?' Her tone was curt.

'Get in.'

He wore a black linen shirt and dark glasses, but even so she could tell his expression was forbidding. She rather suspected she was going to be told off.

'My bus is due any second, and if I miss it I'll have to wait for ever for another.'

'Just get in, Carmen.'

'But I want to go to Santa Monica.'

'I'll take you to Santa Monica,' he said tersely. 'And you and I are going to have a talk on the way.'

'We have nothing to discuss.'

'Carmen,' he warned, 'get in now, or we will have this discussion right here at the bus stop. Either way, *we are going to speak.*'

Carmen looked at the curious faces behind her and then acquiesced, sliding into the passenger seat. One-nil to Elias. But she stared rigidly ahead and tried to breathe only through her mouth and not her nose.

Damn him for smelling so fantastic! Not woodsy or citrussy, just soapy, and so devastatingly sexy that Carmen knew she would do last night all over again—even with the accompanying aches and pains.

'Are you okay?' he asked.

'I'm fine.' She glanced over. 'I still don't want to talk about it.'

'You don't want to talk about anything,' he pointed out. 'You don't say where you're from, you're posing as a stable hand when you're clearly—'

'I *am* a stable hand here,' she protested. 'I wanted a break from riding professionally back home. I came here to clear my head and try something new.' She picked at the hem of her skirt. 'But I missed the horses. I'm not lying. I'm not a wanted felon, or married or anything…'

'I had worked that last one out,' he snapped. 'If you were, it must have been a very unsatisfactory honeymoon.'

He drove fast, oblivious to the glorious ocean beside him, and Carmen guessed he wanted this conversation over and done with.

'You should have told me,' Elias started.

'So you've already said.'

'I'm guessing you're not on the Pill?'

'Actually, I am,' Carmen said. 'I like to know when—' She halted, because this was not the type of thing she discussed with anyone.

Ever.

Sebastián had gruffly attempted to tell her about periods when she was younger, but Carmen had pointed out to her brother that she did work with animals and knew how bodies worked, thank you very much.

'That's good,' Elias said, and she felt him turn and glance at her. 'At least one of us had our head on straight…'

'You think?' Again, she came out fighting. 'We should have used a condom. I'm going straight to a clinic,' Carmen said. 'Not today, though.' She gave a hollow laugh. 'I'm a bit sore. God knows where you've been…'

'Carmen,' he said. 'You don't have to worry about that.'

'Oh, please!' she responded tartly, but was a little stunned when the car slowed and he pulled over.

Perhaps he wasn't entirely oblivious to the view, because he looked out to the bright blue of the ocean for a full moment before turning to face her.

'Listen to me. I've never had sex without a condom before.'

'I have two very corrupt brothers,' Carmen said. 'And I've worked in stables for a long time. I know the rubbish men say—'

'Well, in this instance it's true. I don't have unprotected sex.' He took a tense breath. 'Ever.'

'Then why does it sting when I wee?' she asked accusingly.

'Because I was rough. Because it was new.'

She liked it that he didn't blush, or back off. He went on to tell her that she was just bruised and sore, and that it was normal to be, especially as it was her first time.

'Not that I know much about that, but—'

'You don't sleep with virgins?'

'No.'

'Were you *ever* a virgin?'

He smiled at her loaded question, his first smile of the day, and she wished she could see his eyes.

'Not for long.' Then he was serious. 'Carmen, I date women who know what they're getting into. Who understand that I mean it when I say I don't want to get involved—'

'Then I'm glad you were my first,' Carmen cut in. 'Because I don't want a relationship either, Elias, and I don't want to get involved. I'm here in America to get to know myself better—not anyone else.'

'Fair enough.'

'I have a lot going on at home, and I—' Carmen halted herself. 'I don't want to talk about it.'

'I had noticed.'

'What's the point?' She turned accusing eyes to him. 'We both agree we don't want to get involved, so...' She held out her hands, palms up, and shrugged.

'Agreed, but that doesn't exclude all conversation. Carmen, neither of us wants anything long term, but there's one hell of a difference between commitment and connection,' Elias said. 'We connected long before last night.'

Carmen blinked at the impact of his words. 'True,' she acknowledged quietly, because there *was* a connection, and there had been since the moment they'd met. 'I wanted to come over to you when I saw you outside that night...'

'I wanted you to come over,' Elias replied. 'But we're not dogs in the street,' he said. 'We're capable of conversation. And you should have told me that you'd never had sex before.'

'I disagree.' She shook her head. 'Because if I had told you then I'd *still* be a virgin.'

Yes, Carmen, you would be, Elias was about to say. Because absolutely he should have walked away.

Yet that would make him a liar. Because that was what he would have done *before* he'd met Carmen—before this stunning woman had dropped into his life.

Elias wasn't certain he'd have walked away at all.

'I don't know,' he admitted. 'Maybe.'

When she smiled at his answer, he returned it.

'Can I get back to you on that one?' he asked.

'You may.'

Elias looked at her mouth, and then back to her very black eyes. He'd stopped making out in cars close to two decades ago, so instead he clicked on the indicator and pulled back out onto the highway.

And then he made an attempt at something rather more challenging than kissing.

Getting to know Carmen.

'So, two brothers…?' he asked when his attention was safely back on the road, and she nodded. 'Corrupt?' he checked, repeating what she had said.

'I meant depraved,' she corrected. 'Though not any more. They're both married.' She rolled her eyes. 'You know how sanctimonious ex-smokers can be?'

He laughed, clearly understanding exactly what she meant. 'I do. Joel was the same.'

'I miss just having brothers. Now I have to ask how is Anna, how is Emily? And I'm reminded to call them on their birthdays.'

'Don't you get on with their wives?'

'Yes and no.' Carmen shrugged. 'They're English, and they were best friends before they met my brothers.'

'You feel left out? You don't fit in?'

'I don't want to fit in,' Carmen declared. She glanced over to him. 'Did you get on with your brother's wife?'

'Not really,' Elias admitted, and even if it was a huge understatement, it was more than he'd ever revealed before. 'I never told him, though.'

'But I thought you were close? I've told my brothers what I think of their partners.'

'And how's that working out?' he said drily.

'Not very well,' she admitted. 'But I don't see the point in being warm with them.'

'Warm?'

'Yes.' She nodded. 'I don't want to develop friendships based on the strength of their marriages to my brothers.'

Elias had long since considered himself closed off, but Carmen really was an island, with every drawbridge pulled up and defended.

He couldn't stop himself wanting to prise her open, just a chink—just enough to know her a little more. But that meant opening up himself...

'I didn't tell Joel that I didn't like his wife because it didn't really matter at first. When I first met her she was working for my mother,' he told her. 'I had a big project on—the ranch—and my mother was an interior designer.'

'Was?'

'She hasn't worked since Joel died. Now her main focus is keeping his name alive and staying in with his widow...'

'Staying in?' Carmen repeated. 'I don't understand...'

'It doesn't matter.'

'So, they stay in...?'

'They stay *involved*,' he snapped, certain she must be pretending. He glanced over. 'You have selective comprehension, Carmen. You choose when to understand, don't you?'

'Sometimes.'

Carmen smiled, and when she smiled like that it remained in his head, even as he turned back to the road.

'So she worked for your mother?'

'Yes. I had to go to Europe to do a big assessment, and by the time I got back from my trip she and my brother were about to get engaged and everyone loved her...'

'But not you?'

'Nope.' He shook his head. 'I found her to be...'

'What?'

'Fake,' he said. 'But she was engaged to my twin and working for my mother...'

'What about your father?'

'He adored her and still does.' Elias found he was being more honest than he'd intended to be. 'I did try to tell Joel once. It didn't go down well...'

'Did you fight?'

'No.' He laughed. 'It wasn't pistols at dawn.'

'It would be with my brothers,' Carmen said. 'It was for a while—and they work together. The bodega was not a happy place.'

'Bodega?'

Carmen quickly looked out of the window and he saw her blush, as if she wanted to cover up what she'd just said. 'I think you call it a deli here,' she said hurriedly.

'Take a look,' Elias said, because gorgeous Santa Monica was coming into glorious view, its pier stretched out to the horizon and people milling about.

'Wow!' Carmen groaned. 'How have I never been here?'

'Incredible, isn't it? A bit wild…'

'Wild?' Carmen checked. 'I love wild.'

And even though he could have dropped her off and carried on with his day, he parked. 'I know a nice place where we can get brunch.'

'No, thank you. I want a day to myself.'

She really was like no one he had ever met. 'You're very standoffish, Carmen.'

'No.' She shook her head. 'I'm just being honest. I have one day off a fortnight, and I don't want to have to be on my best behaviour just because I am out with the boss.'

'Since when did you behave?'

'Look, I just want to wander…buy some souvenirs, explore the place. Laura's told me about a few things to do…'

He knew Laura's idea of fun! 'You're not going to see a psychic, are you?'

'Maybe,' she teased. 'I just want to soak it all up.'

'Carmen.'

He halted her, even though he was unsure quite what to say. As someone who knew the pain of loss, knew how vulnerable a person could be in the immediate aftermath of a bereavement, he knew he had to speak up. If she was grieving, she could be easy prey.

'I can come with you...'

'No way!' She actually laughed. 'We have sex once and now you want to come in to see a clairvoyant with me? Do you want the passcode to my cell phone too?'

She made him smile.

'I'll be fine,' she told him.

He relaxed at that. He should leave her be, really. Carmen was right: what she did with her day off had nothing to do with him.

He looked out at the busy street and beyond to the vibrant pier. On the right day it was an incredible place, the best of the best. But on the wrong day...

Or was that just an excuse he was giving himself?

CHAPTER ELEVEN

THERE WERE LITTLE POODLES in tutus, walking on their hind legs, street performers, people on stilts, lovers, colourful stalls and the stunning ocean as a backdrop...

There was nowhere to pause, though. Nowhere to gather her thoughts. It was all music and noise, and Carmen realised her emotions were in tumult.

She leant on the pier and looked at the ocean, but it was as choppy as she felt inside rather than calming.

She had wanted to say yes to Elias's offer of brunch, but she also wanted some time to clear her head. She knew he felt bad about what had happened last night, only there was no need. Carmen had no regrets about what had taken place. She might have been a virgin, but she wasn't a child.

It was her feelings *now* that troubled her.

She had been so sure she could separate her heart and her body, the way her brothers had for so many years.

And yet there was a reason she was twenty-six and, until last night, had been a virgin.

She'd never wanted anyone the way she wanted Elias.

It wasn't just sex. It was the sound of his voice, his scent...how a light seemed to flare inside her whenever she saw him...how somehow she felt as if she shone like a star when she met his eyes...

'Hey, pretty lady!'

A guy joined her as she leant on the pier, and Carmen straightened up and abruptly walked off.

She just wanted a moment of peace, but she was fast realising that wasn't what you came to the pier for.

A woman jogging through the crowd almost collided with Carmen, and she felt an odd flutter akin to panic.

'Slow down!' another woman called out to the jogger's departing back, and then she smiled at Carmen. 'Why would you try to exercise here?'

'No idea,' Carmen admitted.

'Is it your first time on the pier?' she asked.

'Is it that obvious?' Carmen forced out a smile, but it faded as she glanced at the parted curtains behind the woman and saw a table with a crystal ball on it.

'Come through,' the lady said.

'No, thanks.'

'You're worried that he'll never propose...'

'Really, no!' Carmen laughed, and moved to walk away, but she still felt that flutter of panic.

'I see a bull... Taurus?'

Carmen turned back.

'Yes...' Carmen admitted, a little stunned that this woman could know that, but then she gave herself a little shake. 'I really have to go.'

'I have someone who needs to speak to you.'

Perhaps it was precisely *because* Elias had warned her not to that Carmen nodded and went through. Or was it just for the fun of it? It wasn't the type of thing she usually did, but she was in America to have new experiences, wasn't she?

Carmen could feel her own sudden desperation, and an unbearable ache to hear from her father, so she paid and sat down, still telling herself it was just for fun, even though her hand was shaking...

'I see a dark-haired gentleman…'

'For sure,' Carmen said, and pulled at a strand of her hair. 'There are a lot in my family.'

'Sassy!' The woman smiled. 'Now a lady is coming in. She tells me she watches over you,' the clairvoyant said. 'Your grandmother?'

'I never met my grandmother.' Carmen shook her head, knowing this was a stupid idea. And, worse, now she felt foolish, and knew she was being played.

That panicked feeling gripped her as she fought to stay in control.

'She says that your mother worries about you…'

'Well, now I know for sure that you're making this up,' Carmen said, and abruptly stood up.

To her horror, she started to cry. She stumbled out of the tent, blinded by the sudden bright sun and her tears.

'Carmen!'

She was pulled against Elias's chest, enveloped by his scent. Too upset to make a wisecrack, she sank with relief as he took her in his arms.

'Say it,' she said, as she wept into his shirt. *'I told you…'*

'I told you,' he said gently, and then he held her so tight.

Carmen hadn't properly cried since her father had been laid to rest—at least not like this. Or was it that she'd never been held quite like this before? As though he was her shield and she could let down her defences because he would protect her.

'She said that my mother worries for me, but it's all lies—lies, lies!'

'You're okay…'

'No,' she refuted. 'I'm clearly not.'

She pressed her face into his chest and moaned out a sob, feeling as if her knees were buckling, but he held her firmly, and she cried and cried, nestled in his arms, letting herself go…

Really, truly letting herself go.

And there *was* peace to be found on Santa Monica Pier.

It was a comfort she had never known before. And it was beautiful to cry and to be held, not to be hushed or told to be calm, just to be held in solid arms while she cried herself out.

'I'm sorry,' she said, feeling more stunned at her emotional collapse than by losing her virginity last night. She knew she was coming back to herself when she said, jokingly, 'Stalker.' He didn't reply, so she softened and said, 'Thank you for looking out for me.'

'Come on,' he said, and with his arm around her he guided her off the pier. 'Do you want that brunch?'

'I can't go like this.'

'You can,' he said and gave her his sunglasses. 'We'll get a table at the back.'

At a very quiet table, in a cool and shady corner of a beautiful restaurant, she sipped iced water to cool her flushed cheeks while he ordered for them.

'Coffee and…' He glanced over at her. 'Pancakes?'

She didn't nod or shake her head.

'Pancakes,' he said to the waiter.

'With…?'

'Ice cream, syrup…whatever you have. Thank you.'

'I'm so embarrassed,' she said.

'For crying?' he asked.

'More for being such a fool…' Carmen said. 'I can't believe that I was taken in for even one second. She said she knew I was a Taurus, and I am. I don't know how she knew that, but—'

He reached over and took off the sunglasses. When he

saw her red eyes and wet lashes he thought of her lying down with Capricorn. He knew this wasn't the first time since her arrival in Malibu that Carmen had cried, and vowed that if he could help her, then he would.

After last night, he could do at least that much.

'Tell me what she said.'

'Just that… The first thing she said was that I am a Taurus.'

But Elias shook his head. 'What else?'

'She told me if I was worried that a man would never propose.'

'Well, you should have known you were being ripped off right away.'

'I know.' Carmen gave a half-laugh. 'I told her no, and I walked off, but then she called out that I was a Taurus.'

'If you tell me everything that was said, I can tell you how she knew.'

'How?'

'That's what I do at work,' he said. 'I look at all the things that will work, and all the things that won't work, and then again at the things that might… It's risk assessment.'

'It's hardly the same thing.' Carmen shook her head, refusing to believe him. 'You crunch numbers.'

'I do,' he agreed.

'It's not the same as seeing into a heart,' Carmen said.

'It's exactly the same,' Elias told her. 'I get lied to for a living. I get told what's going to be the next best thing, a sure thing, and I get told what doesn't have a hope. And then, if something gets far enough to land on my desk, I get to look at it from every angle. And I'm very good at what I do,' he informed her as their pancakes were served.

* * *

'Well, I don't need some *assessment* to know how she did it,' Carmen told him, as she dived in to the most perfect, fluffy, syrupy pancakes. 'These are so good,' she told him.

But Elias ignored the plate in front of him and sipped black coffee.

'I know she was making it up,' she said, embarrassed to admit it. 'She just took a lucky guess with my horoscope sign—a one in twelve chance.'

'She'd be laughed off the pier in five minutes if she tried to con everyone with a guess. It wasn't some lucky guess,' he told her. 'You try it. What's my star sign?'

'Scorpio,' Carmen declared, because his words stung a little, but he simply stared back at her. 'Gemini,' she attempted, and then flushed, because wasn't that the sign of the twins? 'Sorry, I didn't mean to—'

'Ten more to go.'

'You wouldn't tell me even if I was right,' Carmen huffed.

'Exactly. And that's why your friend on the pier wouldn't bother to try her luck with me.'

'Okay, Mr Logical, tell me how she knew.'

And Carmen told him everything—about how she'd been jostled by the jogging woman, how she'd tried to assert herself by pointing out her hair and scoffing at the idea of a proposal from a gentleman.

Elias said nothing all the way through—just listened. He didn't eat his pancakes. He just drank coffee as she gave her account.

'She called me sassy,' she said.

'Then what?'

'She said something about my mother.' Carmen took a breath. 'But I was already walking out by then.'

Carmen looked at the black linen shirt that had provided the nicest refuge, and then looked up to his chocolate eyes.

'Was the jogger a part of it?'

'I doubt it.' He put down his cup.

'So you don't know?'

'She knew you were Spanish, yes?'

'Not necessarily,' Carmen refuted. 'A lot of people here think I'm Mexican.'

'These are clever people. They know different accents; that's the sort of thing they pick up on. What do you think of when you think of Spain?'

'Home.'

Carmen thought of home, of the bodega, with a moment of such longing that it brought tears to her eyes. But as she reached for his sunglasses again he halted her, and handed her a napkin which she pressed into her eyes.

'What do tourists think of when they think of Spain?'

'Horse festivals?' she said.

'No.'

'Flamenco?' she asked, because that was massive in Jerez.

But he held up his hand in a wavering gesture. 'Try again,' he said, and then picked up his own napkin and held it to the side like a matador.

'Please!' Carmen laughed. 'Not bull fighting.'

'I'll tell you now, if you hadn't lit up like a Christmas tree when she said Taurus, the next thing she'd have tried would have been Spain and bulls.'

'Well, I would have walked off then.'

'When you laughed about a proposal she knew you weren't worried about a guy. You'd practically told her that wasn't what was on your mind. So she deduced that you were wavering about going in because you were grieving.'

'Yes!' Carmen said, seeing it all so clearly now.

'And then, when you got "sassy" about your hair, she took a guess that you'd given your mother some trouble growing up.'

'No.' Carmen shook her head. 'She walked out when I was a baby.'

He offered her a grim smile—the only glimpse of emotion he'd shown since she'd told her little tale.

'She had me at Taurus!'

'Indeed. She could have said the sky was purple and you'd have looked up to check.'

'I hate it that she played me,' Carmen admitted. 'And I hate it that I've eaten all my pancakes and you still haven't touched yours.'

'I don't share,' he said, as her fork hovered over his plate. 'That's why I don't get played.'

Instead, he ordered her some more pancakes.

Brunch after sex was irregular enough, without sharing his pancakes on a Sunday!

'Don't be so hard on yourself,' he told her. 'Grieving is hell.'

'I can't imagine you ever went in for a psychic reading.'

'No,' he agreed, 'but I did talk to my brother a lot in my head, and kept waiting for him to answer.'

'Do you still?'

'Sometimes,' Elias admitted. 'Were you close with your father?'

'Most of the time.' Her breath quivered as she thought of how difficult things had been between them after her mother had come back into their lives. 'We were arguing near the end, but...'

'I'm so sorry.'

'I feel like we're still arguing now. You see, my brothers and I are contesting his will. He's left the family home to my mother, when he always said he'd leave it to me.'

Carmen knew it sounded dreadful, but she did not care what Elias thought—or perhaps she did, because she suddenly found herself trying to explain.

'They were separated for twenty-five years! She only came back when she found out my father was dying.'

'Do you *want* to contest it?'

'My brothers want to. It's all tied up with the—'

'Deli?'

'Yes. The deli.' She looked away as she said it.

'What do you want to do?'

'I want to believe her.'

'I meant about the house.'

He was too logical for words, and Carmen just shrugged. 'I came here to figure all that out. I thought I wanted a break from riding.'

'Your mother?' he asked. 'Did she ever come and watch you ride, or…?'

Elias was trying to gauge just how little contact there had been between Carmen and her mother. It was none of his business, Elias kept telling himself, but with so many rules broken already, what was another one?

'No,' she said, shaking her head. 'I wish she had. My father and my brothers tried to come for the important events, though.'

'You're close?'

'Mainly with Alejandro. We talk most days…'

'So I've seen.'

'I certainly gave *them* a lot of trouble when I was growing up.'

She launched into what she clearly thought was a funny story.

'One time I was told off by the riding instructor. He

suggested, in front of everyone, that perhaps I needed *un sostén*. You know…a bra.'

'Oh?'

'I said, "I thought you were focusing on my riding position!" But really I was so embarrassed. I called Sebastián and I made him go out and buy me a bra!' She gave a little laugh. 'It was not the right one for an eleven-year-old. He didn't know there was such a thing as a sports bra, or about different sizes…'

Elias didn't laugh. He could barely stretch his lips into a smile.

'I wanted her to be there…' Carmen didn't seem to know how to explain her own confusion. 'And yet now she *is*…'

'You hadn't seen her in all that time?'

'No,' Carmen said, and then swallowed.

He got the sense that that wasn't quite true.

'A couple of times…'

Her face was bright red. Elias could almost feel the heat from her blush.

'I'd skipped school. Maths,' she added, as if that explained everything. 'I thought Papá was at work, but I could hear sounds coming from his bedroom. I was honestly pleased, because I wanted my father to meet someone, so he wouldn't be so lonely, but then *she* came out of the bedroom, wearing his robe.'

'Did she see you?'

'Yes. She didn't even seem startled when she saw me.'

'Did she say anything?'

'No.' Carmen shook her head. 'She just gave me this strange smile—I don't even know if it *was* a smile, or just a smug expression…like she'd won something.'

Oh, Elias knew that kind of black smile. He had been

the recipient of it many times from Joel's widow, Seraphina. But to get it from your own mother...

He might not be one for sharing plates, or holding hands in public, but in this instance, Elias made an exception.

He reached over and took her hands across the table. 'I get it.'

'Believe me, you don't.'

Elias didn't correct her. He knew she was partially right—because he didn't know her family, or all that had gone on.

'You didn't tell your father you'd seen her?'

Carmen shook her head. 'Nor my brothers. Though maybe I should have. Perhaps they were long-time lovers...' She rolled her eyes. 'If they were, it will all come out in court. Maybe I should tell them, so they are prepared for it?'

'Well, given you're so vocal to them about their wives,' he teased gently, 'why don't you?'

'Can we not talk about this any more, please?' Carmen said abruptly, and removed her hands.

Elias knew that that encounter with her mother was what had really hurt her.

It was the reason that this incredible, open, confident, beautiful young woman had closed off a part of herself.

Usually Elias resisted deep conversations like this, because they created expectations that he had no intention of meeting.

But, Elias acknowledged, there was a responsibility that came with what had happened last night, and he'd felt her pain when she'd sobbed in his arms on the pier.

There was something about Carmen that meant he couldn't just walk away.

* * *

Elias signalled the waiter for the bill.

Carmen instantly regretted breaking contact.

If she could have done it without him noticing, she would honestly have just slipped her hands back between his, but it was far too late.

'I guess that's why I went into the psychic's tent,' Carmen said, unsure if she was trying to resurrect the conversation or just not wanting their time together to end. 'I wanted answers.'

'We don't always get them, Carmen.'

His voice startled her, hauling her out of her introspection. And as she looked over at him she saw again the man she'd first met at that awards night. Not the terse man who'd refused a drink from her tray, nor even the man who'd stood on stage and talked about grief, desperately needing a distraction so he could compose himself. She saw the man who had leaned against the wall of the venue, staring out into the night…

And Carmen wished—how she wished—that they'd still been holding hands. Because the husk in his tone told her that he might need it more than she did.

CHAPTER TWELVE

VENICE BEACH WAS INCREDIBLE. They walked along the vibrant boardwalk and onto the sand, wandering far enough away that the crowds thinned out.

Then they sat watching the roaring waves and the huge jets in the sky.

'That will be me in a few weeks,' Carmen said wistfully.

'Are you looking forward to going back?'

'Yes,' Carmen said. 'And no.'

She didn't need to explain that she had been lucky enough to have seen many beautiful beaches in her life, but had never sat on one and felt like this before, because she knew Elias felt exactly the same way.

There was an undeniable connection.

And for Elias, who hadn't felt even remotely connected to the world for years, and who could only snatch brief moments of stillness when galloping on an untamed horse, it was like a rare gift.

'If we're putting last night down to a one-night stand,' he told her as he lay back on the sand, 'we're still technically within that window...'

'What window?' Carmen asked.

'This one,' he said, and pulled her down by his side.

It was so good to lie there by his side.

'You scared the life out of me on Dom last night,' he admitted.

'I knew what I was doing. But, yes, I agree. It was a little foolish to take him out with no one around.'

'A *little* foolish?' he repeated.

He stroked her hair and she could see the steady thump of his heart in his throat.

'You are an incredible rider,' he told her.

'Can I take Dom out again, then?'

'You can do some basic work with him, so long as someone else is there.'

She pulled a face. 'Some risk-taker you are!'

'Just basic work,' he said again.

The boring stuff, the repetitive stuff, the over and over and over stuff—that was how conversation usually felt for Elias. An effort. But not of late.

'This beach is more comfortable than my mattress,' Carmen told him. 'Why don't you sort out the accommodation in the lodge?'

'I keep hoping my mother might change her mind and take it on.'

'While you're waiting for that, your staff are sleeping on deck rope.'

He smiled ruefully. 'I know I have to sort the lodge out.'

'Do,' Carmen said, standing up for her colleagues while understanding now that he had hoped his mother might take on the task. 'I'm so pleased I came to Malibu,' she told him.

'So am I.'

'I have the most beautiful horse in the world at home.'

'What's his name?'

'*Her* name is Presumir,' Carmen said. 'It means to show

off, and she does it very well. She's being looked after by a friend while I'm here, being very spoiled.'

'You miss her.'

It was a statement, not a question.

'I feel like I'm having a heart attack when I think of her,' she admitted. 'But I just needed to get away. We have a saying in Spain: *Huye de las personas que apagan tu sonrisa*—run away from the people who turn off your smile. And since my mother returned, since my father died, I'd stopped smiling.'

'So you *were* running away?'

'Maybe,' Carmen said. 'Or maybe I just needed space to make my own decisions…to know my own mind. My brothers are very decisive, but in this case the decision is mine. I don't know why I'm fighting my mother. She's been so much better lately.'

'You said that growing up there were a *couple* of times you saw her?'

She shook her head.

'You can tell me.'

But he paused then, because he understood her dilemma. Wasn't he torn in just the same way? He was keeping his own truths buried deep inside, and yet he was encouraging her to reveal hers to him.

He marvelled at how connected he felt to Carmen; at how he had felt that way since the first moment he saw her at the awards ceremony. Of all people, she was the one he could open up to, wasn't she? The one who would understand?

I won't tell her everything, Elias assured his brother in his head, *but I need to talk to someone.*

He said out loud to Carmen, 'I know that smile.'

'What smile?'

'The one you said your mother gave you. When you saw her coming out of your father's room.'

'How?'

'Seraphina. My brother's widow. When she gets her way, or gets the reaction she wants...' He shook his head.

'You really don't like her.'

'I really don't,' he confirmed. 'And she's everywhere. If I push too hard for my mother to do the lodge she suggests I use Seraphina, because she has her own business now.'

Elias stared blankly at the clear blue sky and knew his face was dark with anger.

'Now she's married a friend of mine—someone from my old polo team. She'll be at the final, and I swear to God...' He swallowed, unable to continue.

'Have you two ever...?' She trailed off, unable to voice the final words and she sat up.

'Nothing like that.'

The look on Carmen's face told him she wasn't sure she believed him.

'You really can't avoid her?' she asked.

'I try to,' Elias said. 'I'm just saying that I know that smile you described, and the damage a person like that can do.'

'Yes.' Carmen agreed. 'Can't you talk to your mother?'

'I've tried. She's not very good at talking about things. She puts on a front...'

'We all put on a front,' Carmen said. 'I am very lucky to have my brothers, because they know what my mother can be like and we can talk about things. Well, argue about things.'

Elias smiled.

'Talk to your mother,' Carmen said. 'Find out how she is feeling...'

'Maybe. What was the other time you saw your mother?' he asked again, changing the subject.

She lay back down and sighed. 'I went to see her when I was a teenager. I wanted to know about make-up and clothes…maybe get closer to her, you know…?'

'What happened?'

'She said I was demanding and needy.' Carmen let out a breath. 'It's true! I am!' She half laughed. 'If you did date, believe me, you would *not* want to date me.'

'So that was it?'

'Pretty much,' Carmen said. 'And then, years later, my father got ill and she returned. I was terrified for him that she'd change her mind and leave—but, to be fair, she stayed.'

There was a pained and careful balance to her words, Elias thought. Every thought weighed out, considered, analysed.

'They were making love when he died. And since he died she hasn't run off. She's still in the house.'

'Why can't you tell your brothers that she was there that day?' he asked, and he felt her body tense. 'What difference would it make now?'

But she chose not to answer. Instead, she lifted her head and looked at him.

'Do you think people can change?'

'Of course they can,' he said. 'But I would never, ever count on it.'

'What do you mean?'

'I don't believe in second chances. People can change all they like, but it won't affect me. Once I'm done with someone, I'm done.'

'Well, *I* believe in second chances,' Carmen said, and removed herself from his arms and lay back on the beach.

'You've already given her a second chance—'

He halted himself. He had no right to interfere with her decision. He had no stake in this; they weren't close enough for that.

He rolled over and went up on his elbow, so he could look at her as he warned, 'Just be careful how many chances you give…'

'Yes,' she said distractedly, and Elias knew she wasn't listening. 'Just kiss me…'

He was the ultimate distraction. This beautiful, sexy man who kissed her so passionately, so softly. And his tongue tasted of the ocean air they were both breathing.

There was no place nicer than Venice Beach if she could be in his arms. He kissed her as if he were stroking her soul, and she felt at peace.

'More,' Carmen said, because his tongue was sublime.

His leg came over her thighs and she brushed his left shoulder, wishing she'd kissed that dark mole just once…

'Don't tell Laura I went to—'

'Shh…' he said, kissing her neck.

'Don't tell anyone about this day.'

'Do you think for a moment I would?'

His hand was on her waist and his tongue was wet and gently probing. Oh, this man…this man who could charm every secret out of her heart and ease the turmoil in her soul. He was so very, very dangerous.

Carmen shuddered. She knew she had to hold on to her heart, because it would not be safe in this man's hands.

'Not here…' she said, but she was weak from his kiss.

How could she be so turned on just from a kiss? So close to coming? He had truly unleashed something inside her, this dangerous, dangerous man.

He stopped kissing her then, seeming to understand her meaning without her having to say it out loud.

They watched the sunset instead. And, oh, it was spectacular. Yet still nothing compared to the bliss of being held in his arms...

But sunsets were safer.

They don't make you vulnerable, Carmen thought as they headed back to the car.

After one last look at the beach as they drove off, Carmen watched the lights from a jet, glinting in the night sky, soaring away from LA.

Soon that would be her...

All the trouble at home was still there, waiting for her return. And she wanted to be ready to face it... Not giddy in lust with a self-confessed commitment-phobe who had a reputation so bad it rivalled that of her notorious brothers.

She wanted to think and to heal.

Not lose herself in his kisses.

Nor did she want to spoil things by getting too close...

Oh, and she knew she would...

Carmen knew she would fall for his charms. She would adore him, and then—because that was what he so clearly did—he would shatter and break her heart.

And his rejection would be more than she could deal with right now.

It was surely better to end things before she was abandoned.

She wasn't a baby screaming in her cot. She was a woman now.

Elias indicated, turning into the white drive that led up to the ranch house.

'Come in and have a drink?' he said.

'Thank you, but I don't think I should.'

She would be sensible here.

He slowed the car to a stop. 'It's up to you, but I have to see to this lot first, then I'll drop you back at the lodge.'

He nodded his head to the horses who were already making their way over to the fence. As Carmen got out the car and joined him she saw they were far from the prime thoroughbreds she had been dealing with.

Well, one was.

'Who are all these…?' And Carmen smiled as she realised she was meeting the Misfits.

There was fat little miniature pony, a very old donkey, and a beautiful roan whom Elias stroked tenderly.

'Hey,' he said to the handsome horse. 'It's night-time, my old friend…'

She watched as the roan sniffed the air, nuzzling Elias's hand. When he turned towards her she felt a huge lump fill her throat as she saw that he was blind.

'He's not used to me bringing guests this late.'

'Then it would be impolite not to introduce me,' Carmen said, muddled by curiosity and relief as she realised that this was not a place he would have brought any of the women he'd dated.

This really was his haven.

'Homer,' he said to the beautiful roan. 'This is Carmen. When I met her she was pretending to be a waitress, and now she's trying to pass herself off as a stable hand.'

'He's beautiful.'

She looked next at the mini horse, and couldn't quite say the same, because the fat pony had her tongue lolling out on one side of her mouth and eyes that were too far apart.

'What's this one called?'

'Gollum,' he said quietly, and gave a low laugh. 'But to her face we call her Pixie.'

Carmen laughed, but soon it faded away. There was

something about seeing his home—the trees and the plants and the Misfits—that reminded Carmen of her own.

'I miss home,' Carmen said as she stroked Homer, wondering what on earth she was doing here when her family was on the other side of the world. Why was she fighting her mother when in truth she had only ever wanted to get closer to her? 'I might head back…'

'To Spain?'

She could tell she had taken him by surprise.

'No! To the lodge.' She laughed. 'But, yes, eventually to Spain.'

'Come in.'

She shook her head, too nervous to glimpse more of his private world. She knew where that would lead.

'No, I have to be up early tomorrow,' Carmen said. 'Today has been lovely, but it's not going to be repeated and I don't want people talking…'

His eyes narrowed just a little. Perhaps he had not been expecting that. She doubted Elias got turned down often.

'I live *and* work with my new friends. We share a house and everything is good—I don't want all that to change.'

'I'm not suggesting you move in!'

'I know,' Carmen said. 'I just don't want to be treated differently by them. And I don't want you to treat me differently at work.'

'I'm barely going to be there this week,' Elias said. 'And why would I treat you differently?'

'Because I'd *expect* you to,' Carmen stated tartly. 'If I was in your bed at night I would not appreciate being ignored the next day. I'd want flowers and dinners and more than you want to give. And how could Blake tell me off if I overslept when I was in your bed? That wouldn't be fair to him. Or to me.'

He looked at her assessingly. Admiringly.

'I'm here in America to make my own way…to work things out… I don't need the distraction of you.'

'Touché,' he said. 'You're okay, though? I mean, after last night, this morning, the pier…'

'I feel better,' she said with a smile. 'I think I overreacted this morning because I felt overwhelmed. I accused you of terrible things…'

'I wish you'd—'

'I know. You wish I'd told you. Thank you for a wonderful day,' Carmen said, 'and a wonderful time last night.' She meant that. 'I don't regret a thing.'

She soon might, though, Carmen knew. If she started to develop real feelings for him.

Hadn't she sworn off even the notion of love? Even dating?

'Night,' she said, and instead of heading to his ranch, where it felt as if her heart was pulling her, she walked across the grounds.

But when she got to the lodge, instead of heading up to her attic room she sat outside in the quiet summer kitchen, thinking about home.

She didn't want to be cynical and mistrusting, like Elias.

Whatever he might say, Carmen believed in second chances, and she desperately, fervently, wanted to believe in love.

Though perhaps not with a playboy…

Decision made, she took out her cell phone and tapped on Maria's name.

'Hola, Mamá,' Carmen said, for the first time since she was a child—not that Maria seemed to notice.

'I am meeting with my lawyer in the morning,' Maria said directly. 'He agrees that you have no right to remove me from the home where I had my babies…where my husband died by my side—'

'Mamá,' Carmen interrupted. 'I'm not going to fight you.' She looked out at the starry night. 'Papá made his wishes clear. He wanted you in Jerez, with your family.' She heard her mother gasp. 'I am going to call Sebastián and tell him to instruct our lawyers to desist.' Carmen took a breath. 'I know things haven't been great between us, but maybe as adults we can do better?'

'Carmen!'

She looked again at the stars, and the beautiful ranch, and thought of Elias and Venice Beach and how cleansed she'd felt having cried. She knew who she was and what she wanted. America had shown her that. No, she thought, Elias had shown her that. It had been absolutely the best night and day of her life.

No regrets…

CHAPTER THIRTEEN

PERHAPS A *TINGE* of regret...

She didn't see him at all on Monday, and that was actually a relief. Carmen didn't know if she could manage not to blush, or light up in his presence. Could she really play it casual?

As well as that, she was fielding irate calls from Sebastián and Alejandro, who clearly thought she had lost her mind.

'It's my decision,' Carmen said. 'I have to listen to my heart.'

'Use your head instead!' Sebastián snapped.

She did not need to be warned, because where Elias was concerned she was frantically trying to do exactly that.

He was a playboy, and he had outright told her he did not want to get involved with anyone...

So why was she regretting not accepting his invitation last night? Why, when she finished early in order to cook dinner for everyone, was she looking towards the ranch and wishing she was there tonight instead?

Why did she droop a little in disappointment when she saw there were no flowers waiting for her...not even a little note pushed under the door?

Anything to show her that their time together had meant something to him too...

But then Maria called, and her heart felt happy. Carmen was confident she was making good decisions in her life, and that made her feel that running away to America had been the best thing she could have done—so much so that she was actually relaxing in her room when Laura came flying through the door.

'We're getting mattresses delivered. Now! You just have to give your permission.'

'Of course!' Carmen nodded, flustered.

'And strip your bed,' Laura said. 'Don't forget to hide anything…' She waggled her eyebrows. 'You know…'

'Like what?'

'Anything you don't want the delivery guys to see!'

Carmen had no idea what she was talking about. Her only concern was getting Laura and the rest of the grooms out of the way before the restaurant delivery arrived…

'Wait a second… I thought you were cooking tonight?' Laura said, pausing before she went down the stairs.

'I'm just about to start,' Carmen replied as she hastily stripped her bed. 'Do I have to do any of the other beds?'

'Of course not.'

The other grooms arrived in dribs and drabs to strip their beds, but finally Carmen had the place to herself— apart from the burly men bringing mattresses…and, better still, new bedlinen for everyone.

Carmen smiled as she peeled the lids off the many boxes of *albondigas* she had ordered, which had just been delivered. She hoped no one would notice the delivery van amidst the confusion of the mattress delivery. She tipped the Spanish meatballs into the huge pot they all used to cook for everyone, then turned the stove to low, and popped the herbed bread into the oven to warm up.

Elias's cell phone number was on the chalkboard, along

with Blake's, for any horse emergency. Carmen tried to ignore it, but it kept flashing at her like a beacon.

While the food was warming up she went to peek at her gorgeous new bed, which was now made up with gorgeous sand-coloured linen. It wasn't exactly flowers, or a note pushed under her door, but she knew it was a little message for her all the same.

Dared she listen to her heart and pursue this…just a little?

She took out her phone, afraid of the pitter-patter of her heart as she composed her text.

Now I won't feel like La Princesa y el Guisante

She didn't have time to look up the translation for him because the hungry troops were already coming through the door, so she closed her eyes and hit 'send'.

Don't let me like you too much, she thought. Or rather, she amended, because it was already way too late for that, *Don't let it show...*

It had been a long day in the office…

Elias hadn't been deliberately avoiding Carmen. God knew there was a mountain of work for him to do in the real world. And yet he'd found himself distracted in a boardroom in Century Park, and instead of arguing with his father about the latest project he'd asked his PA to sort out new mattresses for the lodge.

And now, while it should feel good to be home, as he stroked Homer's soft nose he could hear laughter coming from the summer kitchen, and he felt an unfamiliar thump of loneliness in his chest…

He glanced at his messages as he walked to the ranch and stilled when he saw her name.

He had to look up the translation.

The Princess and the Pea...

Pouring himself a drink, he replied.

What did you make for dinner tonight?

He awaited her response.

Albondigas. Spanish meatballs in a flavourful tomato and red wine sauce with crusty herb bread...

He adored how badly she lied...how she practically recited the restaurant's own menu. He knew it was an expensive restaurant that did not normally do deliveries like this.

He wanted to type, Who are you, Carmen?

No, he wanted to head over there and pull up a chair, laugh with them all into the night...

And then bring her back to his bed.

He glanced at his occasional table and the array of pictures there. There was one he would prefer to smash, or turn to the wall, but his family dropped in now and then, and the housekeeper might talk...

He looked at the photograph of his brother, so proud of his radiant bride, and his face hardened.

That was the reason why he should not go over to the lodge and join in.

That was why he should not text Carmen back.

He would never give someone the keys that would let them destroy his family.

Identifying his twin's body had been a life lesson he had not wanted.

But only immediate family could do it.

'I can't,' Seraphina had said.

His father, grey and shaking as he held his wife's hand, had whispered, 'I'll go.'

He'd tried to stand, but his strength had failed him, evidence of the toll taken on him by the death of his son.

'I'll go,' Elias had said, knowing it would be something his father would never get over. 'I'll do it.'

He'd braced himself not to be able to recognise Joel—in truth, he hadn't really recognised his brother since Seraphina had come into his life—but as he'd walked into that room there had been one faint whisper of relief beneath the grim horror.

His brother's face had not been ruined after all.

'It's him.' Elias had formally identified his twin for the record. 'Can I have a moment...?'

'Of course,' someone had said. 'We're just...'

Outside?

Watching behind a screen?

Elias hadn't cared.

It had been devastating.

Rearranging the sheet around his brother was the hardest thing he'd ever done.

He had not been able to protect his brother in life, but he had vowed to protect him in death.

'You won't tell anyone?'

Elias could almost hear his brother's desperate voice as he replayed, as he had a million times, their final conversation.

'Do you even have to ask? I never would...'

A vow between two brothers.

Twins.

Elias knew how proud of his marriage Joel had been. So he'd promised to take his secret to the grave. But sometimes he felt that in doing so he'd dug his own.

With Carmen he'd found himself opening up, and that would never do…

There was no one better at bland, unprovocative responses than Elias.

Sounds great.

CHAPTER FOURTEEN

ELIAS HAD stayed the hell away.

But by Friday he had no real choice but to go into the yard. It was the eve of the final and he didn't want to leave all the preparations to Blake.

But he arrived to find the yard in perfect calm order.

'Where's Dom?' he asked Blake when he returned from the empty stable.

'In the arena with Carmen, the other dark horse,' Blake said. 'She told me she had your permission.'

'Yep.'

'What is she? Some sort of Spanish horse whisperer?'

'Something like that.' Elias shrugged. 'Who knows with Carmen?'

He walked into the arena and took a seat in the stands. Dom was skipping like a kid on his way to school while Carmen stood in the centre. She had on the yard uniform but had made it her own, with the polo shirt knotted under her bust and her scruffy Cuban-heeled boots elongating her legs.

'Do you want a go?' she asked, smiling and looking up. 'I can show you my technique.'

'I'll just watch for now.'

He could watch her all day, Elias realised.

Could he do this? Could he enjoy the little time they had *and* keep the promise he'd made?

'Are you all ready for the final?' Carmen called up to him in the stands.

'Pretty much.' He looked down at her. 'You know there's a ball afterwards…'

'I told you. I hate things like that.'

'Why?'

'I just do.' She tapped Dom on the rear and he crossed the arena on the fly. 'I like staying here with the animals.' She looked up. 'Well, I did last time.'

He laughed, trying and failing not to recall what had happened that night.

'Come to the ball,' he said.

'I don't have ballgown.'

'I can take care of that.'

'I don't need you to dress me up, Elias.' She stared up at him. 'If I were to go to the ball, I would choose my own clothes.'

'Just offering.'

'Well, don't.'

She was the moodiest, most difficult, intriguing woman he'd ever met.

And stunningly direct at times. For now she looked up.

'Don't you think rumours would start flying if you bought me a dress and we danced together?'

'I'll dance with all the stable hands. Well, apart from John…'

She laughed. 'I don't know…' she said, and clicked Dom on.

But a week avoiding her had been too long and seeing her again, Elias could not wait for the possibility of a couple of dances tomorrow night, so he took out his phone and texted her.

Come over tonight…

* * *

Carmen read it and laughed and then shook her head. She stood, lips pursed, as he came down the stairs into the arena.

He was in his suit and looked incredible. Always lean, he looked as if he'd lost weight in the last few days, and she guessed he must have been training for the final. But when he moved closer she saw dark shadows under his eyes, and a longing in them that had her swallowing down the lump in her throat.

'Carmen...' He took the rope from her hand and secured Dom, and then moved her to the side, his hands warm on her waist.

'Not here...' she whispered.

'Then come over tonight.'

'Elias,' she prevaricated, 'I don't know if it's such a good idea.'

'I do,' he said. 'You know I said I'd get back to you?'

She frowned.

'About whether I would I have slept with you if I'd known you were a virgin?'

'I think we both know the answer to that.'

'Yes,' he said firmly. 'I would have.'

'You would have run a mile.'

'No,' he shook his head. 'But if I'd known I'd have made love to you properly.'

He made her breath hitch in her chest, and she felt herself light up and shine. He kissed her, and she felt ripples of lust course through her as he stroked his hands over her waist.

'Someone might come...'

'Then let's do this tonight.' He looked right at her. 'A proper first date. You can make paella.'

'I'm not cooking on our date!'

'Okay.' He smiled. 'I'll make paella. Even if we're going nowhere, you deserve better than a quick shag on the office sofa...'

'I loved our "shag" on the office sofa.' Carmen smiled at the new word, but her heart was thumping.

These weeks in Malibu had been so healing to her heart...amongst the happiest she had ever known...

She was starting to find out who she was.

The Carmen without the family fortune behind her and the glittering career.

The Carmen who wasn't abrupt and upfront because she had Romero name behind her but because she was simply abrupt and upfront.

The Carmen who had never felt comfortable with any man until Elias...

He didn't even know her real name!

She didn't want anything to change. And change it would, Carmen was certain, when she told him about the bodega, the properties, the jet-set lifestyle, the family feuds...

'I don't want to spoil things,' Carmen admitted.

'We're not going to spoil things.'

She looked doubtful.

'One date. We can do things right for one night. Surely?'

'What about tomorrow?'

'A couple of dances with everyone else around—not exactly a date.'

She stared back at him. For the first time in her life, she felt a wobble of excitement at the thought of dressing up for a ball.

She was listening to her heart when she nodded, even while she was lying to herself when she argued that she wasn't playing with fire, nor at risk of falling in love with this man...

'Do I bring wine tonight?'

'Whatever you want. Do you want some time off?'

She frowned.

'To get a dress for the ball…?'

'If you get out your wallet, there's no date tonight,' Carmen warned.

'It's quite an event, Carmen. I would do this for all—'

'Don't say it,' Carmen warned. 'Just don't. I shall see you tonight at…?'

'Seven.'

'Perfect.'

Elias left the arena.

Damn!

Now she had a date tonight, and a ball to get ready for tomorrow, and she'd declined his offer to skip work.

'Dom,' she growled, 'what the hell am I supposed to do?'

She took out her phone, aching for advice.

Anna… Emily… She scrolled past their names.

Maria.

'Hola, Mamá.'

'Carmen! Cómo estás?'

Her mother asked how Carmen was, but didn't wait for her answer.

'I can't talk for long…'

'That's okay. I just wanted to ask… You know those modern flamenco dresses…?'

'I have just taken delivery of one now,' Maria said excitedly. 'It is silver. My designer is a magician. I was about to try it on when you called.'

'Who is your designer?' Carmen asked. 'I might be going to a ball tomorrow and—'

'Carmen, these dresses take weeks to make. And anyway, you don't dance!'

'I might try.' She felt emboldened. 'Emily took it up.'

'Hmm...'

'I don't know what to wear to this ball.'

'Well, with your figure, maybe not a flamenco dress. Those dresses are better on a woman with soft lines...very feminine, you know.'

How did happiness just squeeze out like air from a leaky old balloon whenever her mother was involved?

'You're in LA!' Maria said. 'Go shopping in Beverly Hills.'

'I'm working.'

'You don't *have* to work, Carmen. I must go. I'm very busy. You take care and I shall—'

'We'll speak soon,' Carmen said, but her *mamá* had already gone.

Carmen was tense, but in a very particular way. Her chest felt constricted, and she hadn't felt that in a long time. Not since she'd arrived in America, in fact.

No regrets, she reminded herself. *It was just Mamá's ways. People don't change overnight.*

'How do I get a ballgown in time?' she asked Dom. 'And shoes?'

She thought of her wardrobe full of outfits at home, but there wasn't time. And anyway, she wanted something new, something *red*...

She did not trust her brothers to get this right, nor their wives.

She dialled another number.

'Capitán?' Carmen said to the captain of her brother's beloved yacht. '*Por favor...*'

She might not have wanted a leaving party on the yacht, but Carmen had a favour to ask, and Dante was the only person she knew who could pull it off.

'Is there time?' she asked.

'Leave it with me, Carmen.'

She let out a breath of relief.

Capitán Dante knew exactly how things should be done. *Exactly.*

Carmen had never looked forward to a date the way she did this one.

She ordered flowers, chocolate and wine, with strict instructions for their delivery. Then she spent a long time in the shower, where she shaved her legs carefully, used a whole tube of hand cream on her skin, and then put her head upside down and blasted dry her hair.

From her backpack she took a black slip dress that folded up to little more than the size of a handkerchief, and some flat ballet pumps she'd bought for her waitressing jobs. She had no bra to go with the dress, so she went without, and pulled on the prettiest knickers she had.

'Wow!' Laura said as she came down the very creaky chairs.

'Hey!' said John. 'Where are you going?'

'To meet some guy I've been talking to online,' Carmen smiled. 'Tell me, do American men expect you to split the bill?'

'I wouldn't if *you* showed up!' John said. 'Though I might if it was Laura…'

Laura laughed and threw a shoe at him, and Carmen knew very well they'd be at it the moment she'd gone— she had the room above Laura, after all.

'Here's my ride,' she said, picking up her bag. 'Don't wait up…'

The poor driver was a bit bemused that Carmen had wanted flowers, chocolate and wine inside the car, and that she wanted to be driven out of the grounds and then back in, this time using the long drive.

She asked him to stop about two-thirds of the way up.

'I have nosey housemates,' she explained, handing him a tip. 'Thank you so much.'

Elias watched her get out of the car. He had no idea how she did it, but she might have been walking into any restaurant in Beverly Hills, ready to be taken straight through to the best table.

Yet still she stopped and gave all the Misfits a treat, and with slavish devotion they accompanied her—on their side of the fence—up the last part of the drive.

Forget *The Princess and the Pea*…he now had on his hands a very sexy Snow White.

Carmen took her time giving the Misfits their treats. She had never needed courage from her friends more.

'I don't want to spoil things,' she said, more to herself than to the oddball trio. 'I have to play it cool and I don't want to get hurt.'

She climbed the wooden steps onto the porch and looked down at stunning mosaic tiling. An intricately carved wooden door had been left ajar, and it was so vast she felt it might belong to a castle.

It opened without her knocking.

'Hey,' Elias said, and she smiled, because that was how he made her feel. He wore dark trousers and a pale linen shirt and he smelt divine—as if two seconds ago he had splashed on cologne. She kissed him on the cheek, because she knew she'd drop her gifts if she met his mouth.

'For you,' Carmen said. 'I don't think men get given enough flowers.'

'True,' Elias said, and looked at the bunch of red roses and carnations. 'Isn't it a bit early for roses?'

'Not for a first date in Spain,' she told him. 'And we love our carnations.'

'Well, thank you. I don't know where the vases are kept…'

'Something smells nice.'

'I told you,' he said. 'I've made paella. Come through.'

'In a moment.'

She stood there, taking it all in for a moment. Carmen had assumed, from the vantage point of the attic, that the ranch building was a couple of storeys high, yet it was actually all on one level, with soaring ceilings, almost cathedral-like, held up by wooden beams.

Carmen was used to luxury, but this was more than indulgence or hedonism. This was both magnificent *and* a home.

Yes, a home.

The distinguished bodega in the heart of the exquisitely private Jerez hacienda she had grown up in was luxurious to the extreme and, despite refurbishments and modernisations, the essence of its glorious past was enshrined in the fabric of the building.

But this…this was absolutely a home, and not even close to what Carmen had expected.

'*Un reloj de pie…*' she said, gazing up at a grandfather clock that told her it was five minutes after seven.

He led her through to the living area.

And, oh, *how* he lived in it.

The magnificent ocean view was its backdrop, but her eyes were drawn to all that made it his. For despite the huge area there were beautifully defined spaces, and the solid redwood floors were softened with silk rugs. The lighting was subtle, yet she could make out a library, as well as a dining area, and her eyes were drawn to a central sunken lounge, with huge leather sofas and winged chairs.

How she'd love to curl up in that lounge, with its fire-places so high she would have to stand on tiptoe to reach the carved mantelpieces.

And yet despite its grandeur and size, despite the art on the walls and the silk rugs scattered on the floor, it was his home.

'Your home is beautiful,' she said.

'Thank you.'

She followed him into the lounge and looked at the central log fire. 'It must be wonderful in winter.'

'It is.' He nodded. 'You'll be pleased to know I've finally persuaded my mother to oversee refurbishments at the lodge.'

'How?'

'I had a long conversation with her this week.'

'Oh!' She looked at him. 'I did with mine too. We're no longer arguing.'

'Great,' Elias said unenthusiastically. He took the stopper out of a decanter. 'Do you want a drink?' he asked, and splashed amber fluid into a heavy crystal glass.

Carmen nodded. 'A sherry, please.' And then she added without thinking, 'Romero, if you have it.'

'I'm not a sherry connoisseur,' he said, and walked over to a bar that would not have been out of place in the restaurant at the bodega. 'But I have this?'

He held up a brown bottle. One that would not be welcome in the Romero bodega.

Yikes!

But she nodded and watched as he went to find a glass.

'A wine glass will do, if you don't have the correct—' she started to say, but then halted as he handed her a very small glass...the type the English would use.

If my brothers could only see me now!

'Why are you smiling?' Elias asked.

'I just…' She took a sip of her drink.

Perhaps he saw the slight pull of her lips. 'Not to your liking?'

She shrugged. 'It's adequate,' she said, then realised how rude that must sound. He couldn't know that the mixed blend was like sandpaper to her skilled palate. 'I mean…'

'Carmen, it's fine.' He smiled and took a sip of her drink himself. 'Oh, that's awful.'

He accepted her. Carmen felt it then.

He didn't know her name, but he knew who she was, and he simply accepted her ways. She could not explain what a gift that was.

Unlike the sherry, dinner was incredible.

A candle in the centre of a beautifully laid table made her ask, 'Your housekeeper?'

'Yes,' he said as he pulled out a chair for her and then brought in dinner—a gorgeous paella with the perfect crust at the bottom.

'You made this?' Carmen queried. 'I don't believe it.' She scooped out a mussel. 'It's almost as good as mine.'

'Thank you,' he said, and they drank the delicious Malbec she had brought.

'So…' He looked at her. 'Am I allowed to ask where you're from?'

'Jerez,' Carmen said. 'It's in the south of Spain and it's very beautiful.'

'And you have always loved horses?'

'No,' Carmen admitted. 'I started riding at four, but it was not until I was a teenager that I felt confident. Honestly, I was terrified of them!'

'So did your father want you to ride?'

'No,' she said, scooping up the sauce with crusty bread. 'Did you make this bread as well?'

'I can't take the credit for that.'

She was utterly certain Elias had used the same restaurant as her, but was in no position to say!

'So, he didn't push you to ride?' he asked.

'No. He wanted me to start dance classes.' She took a breath and decided that this she could tell him. 'My father had sent my mother some photos of me—I think I was four—and she called him and said I needed dance lessons because I was fat...or, as my father would say, *cute*. Anyway, I thought she was going to come and teach me flamenco, and I was so excited. But, no. She wanted me to take lessons from someone else. I was so upset that I chopped off my hair and said I wanted to learn to ride instead.'

'But you actually wanted to dance?'

'Maybe I did. I don't know. Sometimes I wonder.'

'You dance with your horses,' he said. 'I know because I've seen you...'

'Yes.'

Carmen nodded and felt a flutter. Because she wanted him to see her perform, to really see what she could do. She wanted to whip out her phone and show him how good she was—but that would surely only spoil things?

'When did you start riding?' she asked him.

'I was about ten,' Elias said. 'Summer camp. Then later I used to go and man the line at polo, working for the team I eventually went on to play for. My old team.'

'You loved it?'

'I did,' he agreed. 'To the great annoyance of my father. He wanted both his sons in the family business. Unfortunately, only one of them really loved it...'

'You don't?'

'There are parts of it I enjoy.' He looked at her. 'I'd like to take more risks, but my father always wants to play it safe. Joel did too.'

'Oh!' Carmen frowned. 'I thought you would be the conservative one?'

'Why?'

'I don't know... I don't think of you as taking a lot of risks.'

'Carmen,' he said, 'that was you, wasn't it? In the office that night we had sex on the couch?'

'I believe it was.' She nodded. 'That wasn't a risk. I was a sure thing.'

She'd made him laugh.

'And do you not think my walking away from a brilliant career to run a polo yard is a bit of a risk?'

'Maybe,' Carmen said. 'Although I would call it following your heart.' She thought for a moment. 'Do you think your parents resent that it was Joel who died?'

If it had been anyone else asking that question Elias might not have given a polite response, and if it really had been a first date he'd have been calling for the bill. But he was crazy about Carmen, and starting to get her sometimes dark take on life.

'No,' he said calmly. 'My parents were just devastated that they'd lost a son. I've never for a moment thought they'd have preferred it to have been me.' He smiled at her then. 'I do need to talk to my father about work, though.'

'Are you going to leave?'

Ten minutes ago he'd have nodded, but after hearing more about Carmen's mother, Elias knew how lucky he was to have his parents.

He put down his glass. 'I don't know,' he admitted.

'Maybe I can tell him I'm cutting down on some of it. If I could only get rid of that damn scholarship!'

He tapped his forehead in what he had come to think of as *their* gesture—indicating he was fed up to here.

'Win tomorrow, then,' Carmen said. 'Start something you love in Joel's name instead.'

He looked at her and told her the truth. 'You're a brilliant first date.'

'Only because you know you'll get me into bed.'

But not yet. Because tonight they were fixing the world, lying on his couch, eating chocolates, talking about anything and everything, her head in his lap as they listened to music she had never heard before.

'I don't like it.' She shook her head.

'It's romantic…'

She screwed up her nose.

'It is,' he insisted. 'I looked it up especially for tonight.'

'No, it's not.' She took his phone and found something else. '*That's* romantic.'

'Carmen!' He looked at her selection. 'That's a brass band!'

'It's perfect.'

She closed her eyes and Elias knew then that he was in serious trouble. Because one date wouldn't be enough.

Right now it felt as if a thousand wouldn't be enough.

Carmen felt his hand on her face and the music stroking her soul. She never wanted this perfect night to end…

He touched her shoulder, and through the silk slip dress he stroked one breast, till she ached for him to touch the other. But instead she felt the heat of his palm on her stomach, and then the ache of his fingers tracing light circles.

She knew when he lifted the hem of her dress that he was watching her.

'Don't stop,' she said.

'Shh…' he told her, and she felt his fingers slip inside her knickers.

'Take them off,' she told him.

'Quiet,' he said.

And she screwed her eyes closed as his skilled finger slid down and in, knowing just where to touch.

She wanted to call out, but she bit down on her lip, because it felt as if he was drawing invisible threads from her thighs, to her stomach, right up to her breasts.

'If I'd known it was your first time,' Elias said, and she felt his fingers sliding in and out, in and out, 'I'd have done this…'

She was raising her hips to meet his palm.

'With no kiss?' she accused, and opened her eyes. She stared at him for a moment, but then she closed them again to the bliss he delivered, till the thread was pulled so tight that she lifted her hips to a flood of warmth. She knew he watched her as she came against his palm.

'Bed,' he said, and tipped her off the couch.

He led her on shaky legs to places unknown. He could have led her off a cliff and she'd have gone, but instead she got the treat of seeing the master bedroom, with low lights and curtains drawn against the night. Even the bed was turned back.

'Housekeeper?' Carmen asked, as he took off her dress and removed her knickers.

'*I* got the bedroom ready,' he informed her and she felt her throat constrict as he took off his heavy watch and placed it bedside, then he started to unbutton his shirt.

'Let me,' Carmen said, undoing the annoying buttons and sliding the shirt down his arms.

Finally she touched the mole on his shoulder, and his

flat nipples, and she breathed against his chest just to inhale him.

Elias dealt with the rest of his clothes as she explored him with her hands, and when they were naked together for the first time it felt as if a wrong had just been made right.

'I should have kissed you like this,' Elias said, and his mouth met hers.

He kissed her on the lips, so measured and so deliciously slow that she felt as if she might cry...for she'd had never dared imagine that the severe man she'd first met could be so tender.

He took her to the bed, nudging her there with his body, and she held on to his neck even as he lowered her down.

She had to touch his body, to feel his shoulders, his back... She whimpered into his mouth as he gave her his tongue, parting her legs, needing more, needing him, needing *this*...

'If I'd known...' he said, and he entered her so slowly it made her cry out at the exquisite bliss of him squeezing into her.

She closed her eyes to the sound of his breath in her ear, but then he lifted his head.

'Look at me...'

She was too nervous to look at him. Because she knew now that she had loved him on sight, and she no longer knew how to deny it.

'You don't have to hide here...' he said.

Oh, but she did. Because with each deep thrust she felt as if he were approaching her dangerous truth, and she feared she might blurt out that she loved him, wanted him, and did not know how to keep her promise to herself to be the first to leave.

But there was no place to hide as he shifted her legs

higher, and she moaned in pleasure at the new sensations Elias gave her as he moved deep within her.

'Slowly...' she begged, and yet he was taking her faster.

She'd wanted to retain some semblance of control, because she was losing it now. She wanted promises and for ever and for this never to end...

They were way beyond *slowly.*

Her hands dug into his buttocks, every thrust a jolt of pure pleasure as she wrestled with herself, angry at her own devotion. She almost laughed, because his rapid strokes were setting her alight. She was playing with fire and she liked being this close to the flames.

She was the risk-taker, Carmen knew, because she was gambling with her heart.

'Carmen...'

She heard the call of her name and clenched her teeth, maybe to halt her own verbal response, or maybe in ecstasy.

She knew not.

Then she heard his loud, breathy shout and she gave in...just let her body sink into the deep pleasure of intimate pulses as he shot inside her...just caved in, moaning unformed thoughts that he'd somehow dragged out of her.

'No me dejes ir,' Carmen pleaded as he stroked those last drops of pure pleasure into her, and she felt every last flicker before he collapsed on top of her.

She closed her eyes and tried to remember again how to breathe.

Elias lay there. He knew he was by far too heavy for her, but for now he was unwilling or unable to move.

He was not quite ready to return to the soft lights and the bedroom he'd thought he knew, because the world felt rearranged. The grandfather clock was chiming that it was two in the morning, and he felt as if he didn't quite know where they'd just been.

Then he felt her wriggle beneath him, and he rolled off her, still catching his breath—or was it his thoughts? Because he knew he wanted more brass bands and odd conversations in his life.

'Can I tell you something?' she said.

'Yes.'

'Never to be repeated.'

'Agreed.' He was ready, in this moment, to hear anything.

'Every morning I hear John and Laura having sex...'

He gave a low laugh.

'It's my alarm clock,' Carmen said. 'It's all very...' She turned and looked at him. 'I wouldn't like to be in the room above us.'

'Better than the room below,' he said. 'Where do they all think you are tonight?'

'I said that I'd met some guy online.' She told him about the car, and the flowers, and all her efforts to hide where she was really going.

'You really don't want this getting out?'

It was a first for him to be with a woman who wasn't looking for more from him than he wanted to give.

'I don't,' Carmen told him. 'I don't want to change things at work or complicate things for us...'

That much was certainly true.

He still didn't even know her real name.

And even if he somehow understood her reasons for lying, how long till he got bored with her needy, demanding ways?

Carmen lay there, replaying how she had begged as

she orgasmed, and took a moment to be grateful that she'd been pleading in Spanish.

'*No me dejes ir.*'

Don't let me go.

Who said that on a first date?

Or second, or third…?

Surely it was better to leave than to watch it all fizzle out?

'Carmen?' he said, and she turned and faced him.

They stared at each other in a way Carmen did not recognise. It wasn't invasive. It wasn't even questioning. It was, Carmen thought, more complex than that. She'd caught the eyes of competitors before, as they tried to size each other up, though this didn't quite compare…

She had never held a gaze more readily—even if she was unsure of its meaning.

They were gauging each other, Carmen realised, staring as one might into a glassy ocean and trying to fathom its depth.

'What?' she asked to the demand of his eyes.

'I was thinking…'

Carmen dared not hope, because her starving heart might devour this precious moment and misinterpret it as love.

'Why don't I take a couple of weeks off work?' he said. 'After the final.'

'For…?'

'To spend some time together?'

Carmen swallowed. 'What would we do?'

'Find orange sea glass… Have a lot of sex…'

He smiled that slow smile that made her stomach turn over on itself and she knew her heart was screaming for her to say yes.

But her head was yelling its familiar warning.

Do not love him.

The prospect truly terrified her.

'You should get some sleep,' Carmen said. 'You've got a big match today!'

'I'm glad you'll be there this time.'

'I can't wait,' she admitted.

She lay there, awake in his arms, listening to the thump of his sleeping heart, and she desperately wanted to take this chance, to follow her heart…

It had worked with her *mamá*, hadn't it? Taking a risk that someone could change?

Carmen got up and padded out of his bedroom, picking up a towel from the bathroom and wrapping it around herself. She poured herself a glass of icy water from his fridge and walked to the French windows to look at the view.

She moved to place her glass on an occasional table. It was filled with photos, and she picked up one of Elias and a boy who surely must be his brother. Two little boys…one blond and smiling, one dark and scowling…

Carmen smiled when she thought of his wry laugh when he'd told her they weren't identical in any way.

She picked up another picture, an old black-and-white photo of a distinguished-looking man who looked like Elias would maybe thirty years from now. And there went her greedy heart. Because she was *already* thinking of the future, and how she wanted to be part of those thirty years in between…

Stop! Carmen told herself.

And then she picked up another photo and looked at Joel, smiling and proud on his wedding day, and Elias, presumably his best man.

He must miss him so much…

Then her eyes fell on the bride. Seraphina. She'd looked absolutely beautiful on her wedding day, with smiling blue eyes. Carmen saw that the picture was moving. Her hand was shaking as she found out that his secret was possibly bigger than her own.

Seraphina was the woman he'd been speaking to on that first night.

The woman he'd told to go to hell.

It had been Seraphina telling him how much she missed him…

She hastily put the photo down, her head spinning, desperate not to think the worst. But as she went back to the bedroom and dressed quickly and quietly in the dark she knew it was too late for that.

His loathing for his late brother's wife and Laura's comments suddenly made more sense now…

Seraphina had been there at the lodge when he'd suddenly left for a hotel…

'Where are you going?' he asked sleepily.

'I have to be up in a couple of hours.' She was surprised at how normal her voice sounded. 'Go back to sleep.'

'Think about what I said.'

He caught her hand and pulled her in for a kiss, but Carmen pulled back.

'I have to go.'

She left, feeling dazed. His brother's *wife*?

She kept looking for explanations—kinder ones, nicer ones—but her mind couldn't find one that would fit…

She'd been about to hand over her heart to a man who'd had an affair with his own brother's wife.

And then she saw three missed calls from her own brothers, and several messages.

She called Alejandro.

'*Hola,*' she said. 'How is Josefa?'

'Noisy,' he said. 'Have you spoken to Sebastián?'

'No, why?' Instantly her guard was up. 'Is there something wrong?'

'Nothing's wrong,' Alejandro said. 'Well…' He paused for a moment. 'Maria called Sebastián.'

'And?'

'Carmen…she's gone. Owning the property is apparently too much of a commitment while she's on tour.'

Even though she knew her brother was speaking, it felt as the sound had been sucked from the air and she barely made out his words…just snatched little pieces of his conversation.

'Maria wants her name to remain on the sherry label, and in return she will gift you your home.'

'What do you mean, she will "gift" me my home?'

Her voice was angry, mocking, and yet she could feel the sting of tears. It felt like acid raining down on her cheeks and it had nothing to do with money.

'Carmen…' Alejandro tried to comfort her. 'Perhaps she knows we're right and that it's rightfully yours.'

'Please don't.'

She stared out at the night and knew her mother's version of the story was one so many would believe—she was making a generous and magnanimous gesture, letting her daughter have the family home…

No. She'd left. Again.

It hurt no less that in her heart of hearts Carmen had always known she would.

'Are you there?' Alejandro asked.

'Yes.' She looked up at the stars. 'Is Sebastián cross?'

'Not with you. He's worried. He'll call soon and talk through your options.'

'What options?'

'You love the hacienda, the stables…' He paused.

'It was never about that.'

'I know. We miss you, Carmen.'

'I miss you all too.'

'Come home,' Alejandro said.

Right now, they were the only words that made sense.

'Carmen?' Alejandro said, and she turned and looked back at the ranch, and the man she had thought she might dare to trust. 'Carmen?' he said again, with concern.

'I'm fine,' Carmen told him. 'I'm just never listening to my heart again.'

CHAPTER FIFTEEN

'READY FOR THE FINAL?' Blake asked when she walked into his office just a couple of hours after she had decided her heart was closed for ever.

He was updating the huge screen with all the feeds and medications.

'Blake,' Carmen said, 'could I have a word?'

'Of course.' He turned, and then blanched when he saw her red eyes. 'What's wrong?'

'It's a private matter.' She took a breath. 'I hate to let you down… I know I said I'd be here for longer, but…'

'You're leaving?' He frowned. 'Carmen?'

'I can work today…but then I have to go.'

'Don't worry about that for now. Is there anything I can do?'

She shook her head.

'Can I help in anyway?'

'No,' Carmen said. 'Actually, yes. Can I stay back today? I don't want to come to the match.'

She wanted to say goodbye to the horses…especially to Capricorn and Dom.

'Whatever suits you. I'll make a few calls.' He looked at her. 'Carmen…'

'Blake, please.' She didn't want his concern. It might

crack her open to show weakness now. 'I'm just a casual and I can leave without reason.'

'Sure,' he said. 'Of course. I just hope you're okay. The guys will want to say goodbye.'

'Please…' She shook her head. 'I don't want any fuss.'

He agreed, and she went to start her chores for the day.

Blake might be willing to let her go without giving a reason, but she knew Elias wouldn't. She was carrying hay when she heard the ring of his boots and the anger in his stride. She just spread the fresh hay.

'What the hell?' he said, confronting her. 'You're leaving?'

'Yes.'

'And you told Blake and not me?'

'Blake hired me.' Carmen shrugged. 'I don't believe you generally deal with the hiring of junior staff.'

'Carmen!' He took the hay from her and tossed it down. 'Were you going to say anything to me?'

She didn't answer.

'Carmen?' he demanded.

'No.' She shrugged, as if it mattered little. 'I assumed you'd hear. And anyway, we always knew it was a temporary job…'

'I don't get it.'

'Elias, we've had sex a couple of times and that's it. Am I supposed to come to you and give a detailed explanation about why I'm leaving? Do you discard all your women so thoughtfully? Do you give them written warning that you are about to—?'

'Carmen!' He shook his finger at her. 'This has nothing to do with other women and everything to do with us.'

She took in a long breath through her nostrils and looked at the finger he pointed at her. There was a part of her that admired him for coming to confront her.

Her father… Well, he had always just sighed wearily and given in.

And her brothers accepted her demanding ways and simply rolled their eyes.

But here Elias stood, refusing to let her divert the issue.

'I know we're not in a relationship,' he started. 'But—'

'We're not,' Carmen interrupted. 'I don't have to report to you.'

He stared at her for a long moment, to black eyes that had clearly been crying, yet refused to meet his, then lowered his hand to his side, the fight almost leaving him.

Usually he would shrug and walk away. Or rather, usually it wouldn't have even gone this far.

She was leaving.

So what?

Yet in *this* case it mattered.

And, despite her clear defiance, he saw there was turmoil in her eyes.

'Why?' he said. 'Why would you leave now?'

I'm leaving before you lie to my face! Before you hurt me! she wanted to shout. *Before you change your mind and decide I am too much trouble, too much work, or simply tire of me!*

'I have to go.' She went to push past him, but he caught her wrist. 'And so do you. You have your match to get to.'

'I cannot believe you'd do this today.'

She was shaking inside, and feeling so conflicted.

'I'm not your lucky charm, Elias.'

He took her chin and lifted her head, but she would not look at him.

'What the hell happened between me falling asleep and you leaving?'

She looked right at him then, her top lip curling in distaste and then said, 'Take Wanda to the match.' She narrowed her eyes. 'She can be your human shield to protect you from your late brother's *wife*.'

'Nice,' Elias said, and he removed his hand but not his gaze. 'You could have just asked me about it.'

He was icily calm, but his breathing was short and fast and she could tell she'd really hurt him.

'Keep your secrets, Carmen, if they're so important. Carmen from the south of Spain. Carmen the stable hand. Carmen who runs away instead of talking.'

He stalked off, and she watched his back as he went.

CHAPTER SIXTEEN

CARMEN HATED THAT ROW.

Hated every word she'd said.

So much so that when she had the yard to herself she was sick.

'Oh, God,' she said as she threw up.

And as she clung to the toilet she knew, without a doubt, that he would never have done the same thing to her on a day like today. The Elias Henley she knew would have wished her good luck and quietly dumped her afterwards.

'Hello?'

A casual worker had shown up at the yard, because of course he had been booked so that she could attend the match today.

It was perhaps just as well, Carmen thought, her heart hammering as she packed up her backpack, because she couldn't bear to say goodbye to the horses.

All she wanted to do was leave.

Run away.

Only, she'd run away to here.

To the happiest place she'd known. And now she had so badly messed up that she felt as if there was no place left in the world to run.

Carmen wanted to call Maria, to hurl her rage at the

person who really deserved it, but she was out of emotion for her mother today.

Oh, what had she done?

On the morning of the grand final. A match he had wanted to win for his late brother...

She thought about her own preparations before a big event, how she had to have the right boots, the right scarf, the right brush for Presumir...

She could never make that row right. Carmen knew that. But she had to at the very least apologise.

'Good luck,' said Elias's father, shaking his hand. 'Proud of you.'

'We haven't won yet...'

'I'm proud of you whatever the result today.'

'Thank you,' Elias said.

'You're very pale,' observed his mother.

'It's the grand final, Mom.'

Elias could not give a damn about the grand final.

He wasn't angry, he wasn't shaken—he just knew he was in the wrong place.

Carmen was no doubt packing that backpack and heading to LAX, and he was about to play a silly game while she was leaving him.

All the molecules and atoms in his world felt misaligned: the immaculate green grass was too vivid, the world not quite right without Carmen here.

Laura was missing her too, and obviously sulking. 'Carmen would be much faster. Why did Blake let her stay behind? She should be here.'

'Well, she's not,' Elias said, and mounted Winnie, who was so full of energy that he possibly *could* ride her to Vegas...

Their names were being called over the speakers.

'You've got this,' Blake said, as he always did before a match.

'Good luck!' Laura stopped sulking long enough to give him her best wishes.

'Buena suerte!'

He heard her voice and turned to see Carmen, smart in her uniform, her hair in a ponytail. But her face was grey. She was patting Winnie's neck, and although she was looking towards him, she did not look directly at him.

'Thank you.'

I'm so sorry, she mouthed.

But he said nothing, just gave a very brief nod.

And then John caught sight of her.

'Carmen, thank God you're here!' he shouted.

It was the craziest, most dangerous game she had ever seen, and so fast that her head was spinning. She watched them deliberately crashing into each other, and it was hard to make sense of it when her career was one of perfect formations, with beautiful dancing horses…

'I thought it was seven and a half minutes?' she said.

'Plus fouls,' Laura said.

She saw Elias and three others go from standing still into a full gallop, and she felt electricity shoot down her neck…

Far from being a good luck charm, it seemed she had only made things worse. They were one chukka down as Elias jumped off Winnie and changed horses.

'Elias is off his game,' John said, cursing. 'What's going on?'

Elias's team were still down at half-time, but there was barely time for Carmen to register it and not a moment to breathe. There were legs to be unstrapped, tails and manes to be un-braided, and horses to be cooled down.

It was the most incredible, exhilarating game, and she could barely take it in. The crowd was cheering, hooves were thundering, and Carmen could not believe she had ever asked to stay away from seeing this game.

Because she absolutely loved it.

And him.

But there was just no time to worry about her heart, because the opposition had scored again and John declared the match lost.

'It's over… They can't come back from this.'

'Misery!' Laura exclaimed.

There wasn't any time to feel—not for Carmen, as she prepared Winnie for the final chukka. And then Winnie did what horses sometimes did when you were bandaging their back legs and messing with their tails…

'Carmen!' Laura shrieked, and turned the hose on her to wash off the worst of it.

But there really wasn't time to care. And Carmen, who had thought she would never smile again, and certainly not today, found that she was laughing.

'Good God!' Elias said when he saw her.

'I probably deserved it,' Carmen said, and he gave her a brief flicker of a smile.

And then it was all about the match.

'Come on!' John was shouting.

And the line was barely being manned any more. Duties were suspended as they stood cheering on the team, and Carmen watched as Elias charged through the opposition and smashed it.

Carmen started whooping, as she would have done at home.

'They're going to do it!' Laura was calling out. 'Come on, Elias! Go, *go*!'

John was shouting too. 'Go! I think he might... It looks like they might... Yay!'

Then a siren went off.

'They've won!'

Carmen's heart was in her mouth, because it was the most exciting thing she'd ever witnessed. But, oh, it was bittersweet too. Because everyone was so happy, clapping him and supporting him... And Carmen would never forgive herself for throwing him off his game with her personal dramas.

So she put her head down and worked hard with the rest of the staff to rub down the horses and prepare them for transport back to the stable.

And then it was the prizegiving ceremony, and Elias went up to receive the trophy.

'Thank you,' he said in his speech, 'to everyone.'

They all got a mention—his team mates, Blake and his wonderful grooms. But even though he glanced over, he did not look at her.

'Why don't I get a proper mention?' Laura grumbled. 'I'm head groom.'

'And thank you to my parents...' Elias paused for a moment, then, 'We're going to be starting a new venture,' he explained.

He kept it brief, because this was clearly not the right time to announce the launch of something new, and although he did not outright say that the scholarship was being dropped, it was clear that this was implied.

As he spoke, Carmen looked over and saw Seraphina's tight lips. She knew she'd been told.

'My incredible head groom used to teach riding for young people facing challenges...' everyone clapped Laura '...so I'm sure she'll have a lot of ideas, which we'll be discussing. But we want the yard to honour Joel.' He lifted up the trophy. 'This is for my brother. For Joel.'

Vincent was gallant in defeat. 'Congratulations, Elias. I thought we had you, but we'll have to come back fighting next year to challenge you. The win is well deserved, my friend.'

'Wonderful...congratulations.' Seraphina smiled and kissed Elias's cheek, and then turned to greet his mother.

'Eleanor...'

It was no surprise to Elias when she chose this moment to do the most damage.

'We wanted to tell you in person—'

She was about to share the news of her pregnancy, he knew, and Elias had never been more proud of his mother—because she got there first.

'I hear you two are the ones who deserve congratulating!' Eleanor smiled. 'Wonderful news. Congratulations.'

He had found a quiet moment earlier that morning to prepare his mother, and he had also discussed winding down the scholarship fund and starting something new instead. Better to get it all over in one go, he had thought.

Everything was all kisses again, and Elias looked away—to discover that there was no Carmen in sight.

'We're thrilled.' Vincent was clearly delighted at the prosepct of being a father.

'Are you going to ask Elias?' Seraphina prompted him, but then she did it herself. 'Elias, Vincent and I—'

'I hope you're not about to ask me to be godfather,' Elias interrupted. 'I'm far too irresponsible!'

There was a moment's awkwardness, but it was worth the trade, because he saw the rapid blink of relief in his mother's eyes. He was so grateful that Carmen had pushed him to open that door. He could see now that perhaps the strain had been upon her too, and he wished they had spoken about it earlier to save them both some agony.

'Right,' his father said, 'let's head to the hotel. We'll follow you, Elias.'

'I'll meet you there,' Elias said. 'I've got some things to take care of first.'

He found her on the beach back at the stables. She was sitting with her chin on her knees, her face brown from the dust and from Winnie's little gift, and streaked from crying...

'We seem to do better on the beach,' he said.

She gave him a thin smile. 'We do.' Carmen took a breath. 'I would like to apologise.'

'Thank you.'

'Congratulations,' she offered, but he didn't respond. 'They are all fighting for the shower and getting ready for the ball.' She furrowed her brow. 'I thought you were heading straight to the hotel?'

'I was, but now I'm here.'

'I should have told you myself that I was leaving.'

'Have you booked your flight?'

She didn't answer.

'Fine. You don't have to tell me anything.' He shrugged. 'That was the deal we made.'

'You were right about me not giving my mother any more chances. She's gone, of course.'

'So why are *you* leaving?'

'Because of this morning...'

'Come off it, Carmen. You booked your flight before that row. Talk to me,' he said. 'I'm not leaving you like this.'

'I'm hardly going to go to the ball now!'

'Not if you really don't want to, but you can come to the

hotel.' He was being practical. 'You can take a bath, have something to eat—just don't be here on your own tonight.'

'You're very kind, but—'

'Actually, I'm not a very kind person,' Elias corrected. 'I have no issue in not going. They can go ahead without me.'

'But it's your team. Your friends and family.'

'Then come to the hotel. You don't have to see anyone.' He wasn't moving. 'All right, we'll just sit here instead.'

And he was more stubborn even than she, because he ignored his buzzing phone.

'Can I ask you one thing?' he said. 'You don't have to answer, but can I at least ask?'

'I saw Seraphina in their wedding photo.'

Carmen seemed certain that was what he wanted to know.

'I recognised her from the awards ceremony.'

'I'm not asking about her—or that. Why won't you tell your brothers that you saw your mother that day? You tell them what you think about their wives…you tell me what you've decided I've done… You say you can talk to them about everything, why not that?'

'Because I'm ashamed!'

'Why?' He didn't get it. 'Because you heard them having sex?'

'No!' She covered her face. 'Nothing like that.'

'Then what?' His voice was hoarse. 'Carmen?'

'She came home for sex. She came home for her husband. But she didn't come for *me*. Not once. Only for Papá…for sex. She didn't love me even that much.' She held up her thumb and finger. 'I hate her.'

'You love her.'

'Both,' Carmen admitted, and started to cry.

'Come with me.' He stood and lifted her into his arms and held her. She didn't resist.

'I have to get my clothes…'

'And your passport,' he added drily. 'Carmen, I'll drive you to the airport myself, if that's what you want, but I'm not leaving you here upset like this.'

They walked back to the lodge, and for once it was fragrant, with all the soap and perfume in the air, but everyone had already headed off.

'I shan't be long…' she told him.

She went up to the little attic, where her backpack was already packed, and saw there was a large box sitting on her bed.

Carmen Romero
From Capitán Dante

'Ready?' Elias asked.

'Yes.'

He'd already guessed she was leaving, but he knew for sure as they drove down the long driveway.

She couldn't look at Homer sniffing the air… Nor at Pixie, with her short, fat legs trying to catch up with the car.

'I'll just stop and let—'

'Please don't.'

She couldn't bear to say goodbye, Elias realised.

From the basement car park at the hotel they were whisked up by a private elevator to his suite, and he wondered just who she was back home in Spain. Because she had a grubby backpack and also a big, fancy box. She was filthy, and yet as they stepped into the penthouse she managed to smile confidently at the butler.

'Can I get you anything, ma'am?' he said.

'A sherry, please.'

'I'll sort it,' Elias said. 'Could you excuse us?'

A maid came out then, and announced, 'The bath is drawn, ma'am.'

'Gracias,' Carmen said with a smile, but when they were alone she rolled her eyes. 'Why do they assume it's for me?'

'It *is* for you!' He was on his cell phone and firing off texts. 'I might only have time to brush my teeth...'

'Elias, you smell too,' Carmen said, but not unkindly as her ex once had.

'I know. Go and have your bath and I'll be in soon.'

'I'll wait till you're gone.'

'Up to you.'

Only, Carmen ached, and she was so filthy that when she headed into the bathroom she peeled off her clothes and climbed into the lovely, soapy water. She knew she was a coward for not telling him that she would be flying home *tonight*. But she had never learned how to say goodbye, and she still didn't know how.

To people.

Or to horses.

But especially to him.

Elias's phone was lit up like a Christmas tree, but he made only a few quick calls as he sorted out his suit.

He glanced again at the backpack and the box...

Carmen Romero

So that was her name, was it?

He poured her a drink, and now he saw it was Carmen's phone that flashed a message, inviting her to check in for her flight.

Her flight *tonight*.

First class!

Well, that explained a few things...

* * *

'Here.' Elias came in with a bottle and a proper sherry glass. 'That sherry you like.'

'Oh!'

'Is it adequate?' he quipped.

'Perfect,' she said, and then blushed. 'You saw my name on the box.' She turned the bottle so the image of her mother faced away. 'My full name is Carmen Romero de Luca.'

'And the bodega's not a little corner deli, I take it?'

'No…' She gave a soft laugh. 'That is my mother on the label.' She watched him glance towards the bottle. 'She would like to remain there. My oldest brother disagrees.' She shrugged. 'That's the next legal battle.'

'Yikes…'

'And then we shall have nothing left to fight over.'

'Oh, there'll be something. There's always something.' He looked over at her, naked in the bath. 'I'm going to tell you something that I swore I never would tell a soul. I made the promise to my brother when I identified his body—'

'Please don't break your promise because of me.'

'I want to,' he admitted. 'I trust you.'

'How can you after this morning? And when I've only just told you my real name? I haven't been honest all along…'

'You haven't lied, Carmen, you just haven't opened up.' Elias paused and looked at her again, lying stretched out in the bath, and then he amended that. 'Fully.'

Carmen wasn't sure she was up to any confessions right now. She didn't think she'd be able to say the right thing. But then she looked at the trouble swirling in his velvet brown eyes. Even if what Elias told her wasn't what she wanted to hear, the very least she could do was listen. She looked at Elias—really looked at him—and knew that it wasn't just about trusting another person, but about trusting yourself also. Trusting that you would do your best, even if faced with something that wasn't what you wanted, because you cared so very much.

'You can tell me.' She gave a small nod.

'Seraphina…' He swallowed and his voice was hoarse. She could see his guilt and his agony.

'Okay…' Carmen said, in a voice that was gentle rather than shaking with fear, even if she was more terrified than when she'd first turned her back on Domitian.

'A couple of weeks before Joel died, she came on to me…'

Carmen actually wanted to stand up, climb out of the bath and walk away before he revealed what she knew was coming, but she owed it to him not to flinch or show fear…

'I was staying at the lodge, and she was there, measuring up something or other. I didn't even know she was there. I came out of the shower, heading up to the attic, and she was on the stairs…'

Carmen could picture it exactly…knew the squeak of every stair between the bathroom and the little attic bedroom. She lay so still that the water didn't so much as ripple, yet she felt as if she was being pulled into his hell.

'Nothing happened. I pushed her away. I was so shocked, and I might have been a bit rough…'

Carmen felt as if the oxygen masks had fallen down on a plane, but she was too scared to reach for one in case the motion betrayed her terror. Now she was afraid that he'd find out she'd believed the very worst of him.

But, given her cruel words this morning, he already knew that.

'Elias…' She touched his arm. 'I am so sorry for what I said.'

'Carmen, I get it. I would have thought the same. But

nothing happened. At first I was so shocked that I couldn't move. She said it had always been me...that Joel would never have to know.' His voice really was hoarse now. 'She was his *wife*. He was my *twin*. I mean...what the actual hell?'

'You didn't tell Joel?'

'Hell, no!' He shook his head, and then he looked at her with eyes that showed he had wrestled with that question all alone for so long. 'Should I have told him?'

'How could you have?' She thought of her brothers in that situation. 'No, you couldn't tell him. Have you told *anyone*?'

'You.'

She heard the single word.

Not, *Just you.*

Just, *You.*

'Joel called me on the night of his accident. He was a mess...crying. He said that since they'd got back from their honeymoon things had changed between him and Seraphina. He was asking for my advice. I just told him to give it time...that marriage couldn't all be a honeymoon. He agreed—he even laughed. He asked me not to tell anyone that he'd had doubts.'

Elias buried his head in his hands.

'I swore I wouldn't. And then...then I heard the accident...'

It felt as if the hot water she lay in had risen to a boil... as if the steam had taken the oxygen from the air as she glimpsed his hell.

Carmen asked the bravest question. '*Was* it an accident?'

'Yes!'

He pulled his head from his hands and looked at her. He nodded, certain.

'I heard it all happen, and when I got there I found out

that a truck driver had crossed lanes. It turned out he'd been drifting for a few miles and had fallen asleep. Joel was on his cell phone... Both of them were in the wrong...'

He took the hand that was resting on his arm and toyed with her fingers. He turned her hand over and looked at her palm.

'You have a long lifeline.'

'You don't believe in all that!' Carmen joked, but she knew he was just taking a moment...focusing on the irrelevant for a moment before diving back into hell.

'I made a decision to keep it all to myself,' Elias told her. 'Once it was clear it had been a dreadful accident, I didn't see the benefit in telling anyone the content of our conversation, or about what Seraphina had tried to do.'

'Why?'

'I didn't want to hurt my parents any more than they already were. But mainly for Joel...because he was so proud of his marriage. He loved her... When I went to identify his body, I swore to him that I'd take it to the grave...'

'Some secrets need to be shared,' Carmen said.

'Yes, they do.' He nodded. 'Carmen, I'm not saying this just for me...' He looked at her. 'I'm not unburdening myself out of guilt. I'm telling you this because of what you told me. Your brothers should know. You have nothing to be ashamed of. It's her shame, not yours.'

'I'm sorry I left you like that.'

'Just try asking me next time.'

'I asked you about Wanda,' she pointed out.

'We weren't together then,' he said. 'Anyway, you've got a first-class ticket out of here, so you don't get to hold that over me.'

'How do you know that?'

'I was going through your phone,' he teased, then gave

her a look that told her it was a joke. 'I saw the message flash up.' He stood up. 'I have to get ready for the ball now.'

'I know. Will Seraphina be there?'

'Yep,' he said, stripping off. 'Trying to get a moment alone with me, no doubt.'

'I'd love a moment alone with Seraphina,' Carmen muttered. 'I would finish her.'

'You probably would!' He snorted, smiling.

She watched him turn on the huge shower in the centre of the bathroom, but then he came over and picked up the sherry bottle.

'What are you doing?' she asked.

'Putting your mother outside while I get naked!'

It made her laugh, and she lay watching him stand beneath a cloud of water, soaping his chest, his underarms, and then he looked at her and soaped his stomach...and then lower.

It would be so easy to climb out of the bath and go over and hold his lovely soapy body...

'Thank you for bringing me here with you...'

'Thank you for coming.'

She watched as he brushed his teeth and picked up the brush to soap his face before shaving. And then she was out of the bath and running her fingertips over that mole.

Her hands closed around the shaving brush. 'Let me.'

'I am not letting you shave me!'

She soaped his neck, and a little of his jaw, and then they sank into toothpaste kisses. She felt her damp body so receptive to his.

'Careful!' he said as she kissed his neck. 'I have to look nice tonight.'

'You always look nice,' Carmen said, kissing his chest and his flat nipples.

Her hands slipped down to the curly hair on his stomach and then she held him.

'Yes…' he groaned.

'You'll be late…'

'Do I look like I care?'

He nudged her legs apart and brushed his fingers over her dark triangle, parting her intimate lips. She'd never seen herself so pink and turned on before.

Carmen held on to the marble counter, and watched as he shifted her bottom right to the edge. She bit down on her lip as he took his time, slowly nudging in.

'More…'

'Just watch,' he told her, and she could not believe she didn't feel shy as they watched together.

When it was time, she looked at him instead, and let him take her to the places only he could, right there, on the marble countertop, pressing into her again and again and again.

And she did not want them to ever end.

'I've got to go,' he said as reluctantly led her through to the bedroom.

'I know.' She lay back on the bed and watched him dress. 'You still have to shave…'

'Too late.'

He was doing up his tie.

'So what else haven't you told me?' he joked as he pulled his jacket on.

'I'm rich…'

'Brilliant.' He smiled. 'What else?'

'I'm a better rider than you.'

'Ha!'

'I can't cook…'

'Neither can I!' He laughed. 'Nothing else?' he checked.

What should she say? Did she dare to tell him she loved him?

'Carmen, I know your flight's at midnight…'

Carmen pressed her lips closed, relieved she hadn't bared her heart…

'So this is goodbye?' he said.

She nodded.

'Here.' He went to the bench and picked up his wallet. 'I was going to give you this later.'

He took out a dark stone and handed it to her.

'Sea glass!'

'*Orange* sea glass!' he said.

'Brown,' Carmen corrected, and then realised how ungrateful that sounded. 'But I love it. I really do…' She fell silent as he turned on the overhead light. 'Oh!'

It really was orange. Well, maybe…at a push. It was a dark, golden orange—a colour her beady eyes had scanned every beach for.

'Do you know how rare this is?'

'Yep.'

'I mean it, Elias. This is seriously rare.'

'Very,' he agreed. 'And so is this chance…'

He took her chin and looked right into her eyes, but if she couldn't quite look back at him.

'Why *are* you leaving tonight, Carmen?'

'I have things to sort out at home.'

'That's an excuse.'

'It's my home,' she attempted, but he would not let her hide. 'I've got a family at home who loves me.' She could hear her own plea for guarantees and hated her desperation. 'If I stay here and we get closer, it will make it harder to leave…'

'It's the same for me.'

'No…'

'Yes.'

He picked up the sherry bottle and looked at the dark-haired woman on the label and the swirl of her orange flamenco dress. He took out his pen…

'Don't!' she warned as he scribbled on it. 'Don't erase her.'

She went to reach for the bottle, angry at his disrespect, but he turned wide shoulders to her.

'That's my *mamá*!'

'I know.' He took a swig of sherry from the bottle and pulled a face. 'You're right. Maybe we could never work. That's dreadful…'

'Hey!' Carmen warned as he grimaced, but then she smiled.

He spoke in Spanish then. '*Huye de las personas que apagan tu sonrisa.* Run away from the people who turn off your smile.'

Carmen frowned, wondering if he'd misunderstood what she'd been trying to say that day…if somehow the translation had been lost.

But no.

'I turn on your smile, Carmen, and you know it. So why would you run away?' he asked, and then he shrugged. 'I might see you later.'

And then he walked out. And the only indication that he was angry was the silence he left behind.

If he loved her, he'd stay, Carmen decided.

But she knew that wasn't fair.

There was a ballroom full of people waiting for him.

She was sick of running away…

And she could not stand for this to be goodbye!

The *capitán* of her brother's yacht was used to demands from his spoilt guests—and Carmen had been one of those on many occasions. And yet there was so much care wrapped up in this package, because he had sent her favourite red velvet dress.

Perhaps he had spoken to her brothers? Or had he relied on a memory?

Also in the package was her eighteenth birthday present from Papá—gorgeous diamond earrings—as well as her twenty-first birthday present—a necklace, also from Papá…

There was nothing, not even a hairpin, from Maria. Not even a card.

There was, though, a card from her sister-in-law Anna…

Capitán Dante asked for some help with the underwear! I remember you taking me shopping once. I hope these are to your taste, Anna x

Carmen laughed, and then looked at the X, the little kiss from her sister-in-law. They'd gone out dancing once, and had got on well, yet Carmen still held back, also with Emily…

There was another package, a small one, containing red lipstick from Emily.

Her favourite, the note said, rather cryptically. And another X.

Were they her family?

She wanted to dress up, to dance, to truly be Carmen Romero…

Carmen blasted her long black hair dry, and then combed it smooth.

Again she was grateful that she always wore gloves when working in the stables. Her nails might not be done, but her hands were always ready to go out, presenting the Romero brand.

She pulled on the brand-new lilac underwear, and then the long dark red gown and high-heeled shoes…

She would be herself tonight.

Her new self.

Usually she loathed all this, but tonight she was shaking with excitement...

Carmen poured another small sherry, to raise a glass to Papá, but then she saw that Elias hadn't been scribbling a moustache or scratching out her mother's eyes. Instead there was some writing on the bottle.

I want to dance with Carmen.

She scanned the label, looking for a little love heart, a clue, even a moustache on her *mamá.*

There was no hate in his words. No ultimatum. No threat. No challenge. No comparison or competition.

Elias Henley wanted to dance with a woman who insisted she didn't want to...

But desperately did.

Carmen looked in the mirror at her rather too tanned shoulders, and possibly too muscular arms, and then she took out the lipstick from her sister-in-law and painted her full lips red.

She picked up her phone to text Seb and tell him she was ready to take things from here, but she didn't want that tonight...

Alejandro, maybe. She would tell him she would not be heeding his warning about a certain playboy...

Then her mind flicked to Maria, to her *mamá.* No, her mother wouldn't be excited for her tonight...

So she started a new group: Carmen, Anna, Emily... And she attached a photo of herself in her velvet gown, her diamonds, and her red lips with their very wide smile.

Allá voy. Deséame suerte!

Then Carmen had a little panic. Because she'd written, *Here goes. Wish me luck!* in Spanish, and they were, of course, both English, and she didn't want them asking her brothers to translate.

But the replies were instant...

Hearts.

Shining eyes.

Kisses and best wishes.

It made her feel braver to know she had them on her side.

Putting down her phone, she took one more breath and looked in the mirror—and there she was.

Carmen.

Who just happened to love Elias—the man who turned on her smile.

And if it didn't work out...?

Instead of running from the thought, she faced it. Faced herself in the mirror.

'You'll survive,' she said aloud.

CHAPTER SEVENTEEN

'WHERE'S WANDA?' asked his mother, when she saw Elias was attending one of these functions for the first time without a date.

'We broke up,' Elias said, offering no more than that.

'Darling…' Eleanor said. 'You didn't say!'

He took a drink and all he could think about was Carmen…that she might right now be in a car on the way to LAX.

He could not understand why Carmen was leaving tonight…how she could walk away from such promise and hope… But his mother was giving him a tiny smile, a supportive smile, and although she was difficult at times, even through hard times Elias knew she had always loved him.

He would never take her for granted.

'I am sorry…' Eleanor sighed. 'How long were you and Wanda…?'

'It's fine.'

'I knew there had to be a reason.' Eleanor sighed again. 'You haven't even shaved…' Then she smiled at him. 'Well done again for today!'

'Thanks.' He looked at his father, and then back to his mother, and knew how lucky he was. 'It means a lot that you're here.'

'Of course,' his father barked, and even though William Henley loathed the way his son's passion had taken him away from the family business, he was still here, supporting him.

Elias went over to join some of his teammates, and right on cue, Seraphina made her way towards him. 'I just heard about you and Wanda.'

Elias said nothing. Refused to react.

'I thought you'd been a little off lately…'

Seraphina spoke in a little girl's voice at times, and if there was one thing he couldn't abide it was grown women doing that.

'What happened?' she asked.

She put a hand on his arm and Elias wanted to brush her off, or get in some dig about how he'd met someone else, someone with integrity… He wanted to turn and look into her Machiavellian eyes and tell her he'd found love…

But there was someone else who deserved to hear that first.

Needed to hear that, perhaps.

Of *course* Carmen wanted guarantees, Elias realised—she was terrified to bare her heart.

'Excuse me, but I really need to—'

He was going to leave and to hell with the speeches. If Carmen had left already, then he'd head straight to LAX.

But even as his decision was made there was a stir in the room…

'Look at you!'

He heard Laura's incredulous voice and he turned.

And there was Carmen.

She certainly did not need a trip to Beverly Hills with his credit card…

Her black hair was gleaming and there was dark red lipstick on her sultry lips, and even though she hadn't so much as looked in his direction she wore a smile that he knew was just for him.

'Who's that?' Seraphina exclaimed.

Elias didn't even answer her. For five years now he'd been trying to come up with the right words to say to his ex sister-in-law, but there were two little words that came easily tonight.

'Hold that.'

He handed Seraphina his glass, then made his way over to the undisputed belle of the ball, who was now standing with her colleagues and friends.

'Look at you, Carmen!' Laura was beaming. 'How did you get that dress in a backpack?'

'Well,' she said in her rich throaty voice, 'it's best to be prepared...'

He didn't know how she'd managed it, but he did know it had taken every last nerve she had to walk into the ball.

After a lifetime of rejection, she had chosen to risk her heart to him.

He would never, ever let her down.

'You look incredible,' he told her.

'So do you.'

She put her hand up to his jaw. He didn't pull his head away because this was no feigned affection.

'You still haven't shaved?'

'I was a bit busy...' He looked at her shining black eyes. 'Did you get my message on the bottle?'

'That's why I'm here.' Carmen smiled. 'To claim my dance.'

On this beautiful night the ballroom lit up, and she leant on his chest and danced in his arms.

'Thank you for not leaving tonight...'

'We deserve a chance.'

'We're more than a chance,' Elias said. 'I love you.'

'Don't say that just because you've won today or—'

'I love you,' Elias told her again.

'Never take that back.'

It was an odd response, perhaps, especially from someone who looked so confident and poised. But he took her plea seriously, and understood that her doubts came from a world before him.

He said it a third time, right into the shell of her ear. 'I'm going to love you for ever.'

CHAPTER EIGHTEEN

CARMEN HAD THOUGHT—or rather she'd been told since she was a little girl—that she would marry in Jerez and her father would give her away.

'I always thought I'd have a reception at the bodega, like you did,' she said to Emily, who was taking her wedding dress out of its reams of tissue paper. 'I don't know what Papá would say about a wedding in Malibu!'

'I think he'd be thrilled to see you so happy,' Anna said.

'We couldn't leave Dom, you see. Not when he's doing so well. It would really have set him back…'

Her voice trailed off. Her brothers and their wives had all been a little baffled and trying not to be when she'd explained that they couldn't leave Dom just now.

After all, Anna had left her daughter, Willow, to attend Emily's wedding.

She smiled now at Willow, her bridesmaid—she was officially her niece now, because the adoption had finally come through.

'You look like a flamenco dancer,' Carmen told her.

'I *am* a flamenco dancer!' Willow exclaimed.

And then she looked at Emily, who was holding Josefa.

They seemed like sisters, even if they didn't quite understand each other yet.

They were there for each other.

Her family was here in Malibu for this very special wedding.

In a few weeks they would take a honeymoon in Jerez, and sort out the transfer of Carmen's horses to Malibu... For now, though, it was all about today.

It had been four weeks since Elias had told her that he would love her for ever. Four weeks of drama. Because when Sebastián had heard she was engaged to marry he'd been all set to board the next flight...

Anna had talked him down.

Alejandro had been stuck at home with the lawyers, battling Maria, but Emily and little Josefa had come out early, the week before the wedding, and helped get things ready.

Their wedding was to take place on the ranch, but with such a rushed event the numbers were still a little up in the air, and even on the day of their wedding there were still responses to come.

'She hasn't even responded,' Carmen had said, when Elias's assistant had confirmed last week that Maria had failed to RSVP. 'It was such short notice, though. Knowing Maria, she might just turn up at the last minute and surprise everyone...'

Then her voice had faded. She doubted she'd come, but was still hoping she might...

'It's fine,' Elias had said. 'There's plenty of room if she does come.'

'In the attic!' Carmen had snapped, though the barb hadn't been aimed at him.

'No, I've kept one of the guest suites for your mother. She's always welcome in our home...'

He accepted that Carmen loved her, even if it could never, ever work out.

'Guess who *has* responded?' Elias had gone on. 'Seraphina and Vincent can't come.'

'Oh, that's a shame…'

'They're off on a babymoon—whatever that means. It was booked as soon as they found out they were expecting, apparently.'

'Oh, well…' Carmen had said, and then had turned away so he wouldn't see her sudden blush.

'What *is* a babymoon?' Elias had asked.

'A holiday before the baby comes…'

And now their not very long-awaited wedding day was here.

Carmen sat in a robe, her black hair slicked back into a low bun. Though Emily had tried, Carmen took over and tied a large red silk rose to the base of the bun, so it sat at the side.

'Ready for the dress?' Emily asked.

'One moment,' Carmen said, and slipped into the en suite bathroom.

As she turned the lock she stood for a moment, looking at one of the drawers and knowing what she'd hidden there. She'd bought the pregnancy testing kit yesterday, and had been telling herself to wait until tonight, or tomorrow, or…

Except she had no patience!

Carmen stood there, hearing Willow laughing and little Josefa singing, and her sisters-in-law chatting in the bedroom as she watched the lines appear and found out that she was to be a mother.

There was no fear, nor any worry as to what Elias would say.

Their love might be new, but it was by far too certain for her to worry about that.

Just for a moment, as she found out she was to be a

mother, she wished she had her own mother to share it with. But then the string quartet started playing, and she peered out of the window to see the gathering congregation.

Carmen knew that she had a village to support her...

More than that, soon she would have a family of her own.

Both Sebastián and Alejandro walked her towards Elias. The brothers who had argued with her, parented her, loved and supported her and would never let the miles separate them from her took her arms and walked her down the aisle to the delicious strains of the quartet.

There were so many smiling faces in the congregation, but they were all a bit blurry for Carmen.

Her focus was on him alone.

'Carmen,' Elias greeted her. 'You look wonderful.'

She wore a little bit of home—a modern ivory Flamenco dress and a shawl—because even if she'd rejected it out of hand flamenco was something she secretly loved too.

Elias looked incredibly handsome, in a charcoal-grey tailored suit and a silver tie, and she put her hand up to his freshly shaved chin and loved the way he captured her hand and held it there. That was all it took to know they were real.

It was gorgeous and low-key.

There was some beautiful music, and the celebrant told the congregation a little of their story.

'Elias and Carmen didn't actually meet here,' she told everyone. 'Carmen was waitressing...'

She spoke about those who were absent, about Joel and José, and Carmen looked up and saw the only tear she had ever seen in the darkness of his eyes.

'Carmen and Elias miss them today and every day,' the celebrant said on their behalf.

That would always be true.

'And now they've written their own vows...'

Elias went first. 'Carmen...'

He took her hands. He'd been thinking about what to say for four weeks. He'd spoken with his mother, her family, and he'd read books. He'd thought of the many weddings he'd been to and now he had quite a speech written in his head.

But then he looked at her waiting eyes and he thought of her standing in her crib as a baby, needing and demanding love...

'Carmen, I love you,' he told her. 'I want to walk with you and our horses and I want to dance with you, and I can't wait to go to Jerez and learn to love sherry...' He saw her smile. 'But first, last and always, I love you. That will never change.'

'Thank you.'

'Carmen?' The celebrant prompted.

'Elias...' Carmen took a breath. *'Eres el amor de mi vida...'* He squeezed her hand. 'You are the love of my life. I've waited so long to meet you.'

Their rings were simple—Californian gold for Carmen and Spanish gold for Elias—and they slipped on easily. Then Elias took out another ring—the gorgeous orange sea glass he had found on the beach and had had set in delicate gold.

Well, it was more brown, although neither would ever actually admit it, and they would keep looking for a true orange one.

Elias didn't wait to be told he could kiss his bride, and Carmen closed her eyes in bliss as his mouth came down on hers...

* * *

'I don't understand...' Eleanor Henley was on her second glass of Romero sherry and trying to work out how Spanish surnames worked. 'So you keep the father's surname and drop...?' She looked up as Carmen came and sat down. 'So you'll be Carmen Henley Romero?'

'No.' Carmen shook her head. 'I'm going to be Carmen Henley, but professionally I will stay as Carmen Romero.'

Carmen was holding little Josefa, who was standing on her lap. She had grown so much in just a few weeks.

'She's trying to stand already.'

'She's making up for being early,' Emily said and smiled.

'Have a drink,' Sebastián said.

But Carmen shook her head. 'I'm sticking with water...'

'No, look.' Sebastián pushed the sherry bottle forward, and then looked at his sister. 'Look at the bottle.'

'What?' Carmen said, and then shook her head. 'Let's not talk about the label today...'

'Just *look*!'

She turned it around and there, dancing on the label, was her *mamá*. But on the other side was Carmen, in a print out of a photo taken just now on the dance floor, her white dress swirling, utterly happy and free...

Maria might not like sharing the spotlight, but in Carmen's eyes they were finally dancing together...

'I love it!' Carmen smiled and clapped her hands.

'Me too,' Emily said and then gazed at the dreamy view. 'It's so beautiful here.'

'It is,' Carmen agreed. 'Though, I can't wait to show Elias around Jerez, I think we will be spending a lot of time there—especially for the horse festival.' She looked over to Anna. 'How's the new home?'

Sebastián and Anna had taken over the hacienda, and

it was perfect for their little family. Willow was delighted by her life and being spoilt rotten by Carmen's, oh, so strict brother...

Carmen's niece had a wonderful new adoptive father. Yet as a brother he was still protective, and still looking out for Carmen.

'Why,' he asked, 'is your new husband on his phone on his wedding day?'

Carmen looked over and saw a flash of concern cross Elias's features. She knew the only reason he'd be gazing at his phone today.

Handing Josefa back to Emily, she went over. 'Capricorn?' she checked, and looked at the video. The mare was pacing the stable—and not in the way she did when she was tired...

'I'll let Blake know,' Elias said, but Blake was enjoying the party, and anyway Carmen was already walking towards the stables.

'This is *not* how you're supposed to be spending your wedding day!' Elias said as they entered the stable...

'It's the perfect way,' Carmen said, holding Capricorn's neck and soothing her. 'We're here, darling...'

'She's close,' Elias said. 'Where's the vet?'

'Up to no good with one of the grooms, I should think!'

'Carmen?' He looked over at her. 'Do you have something to tell me?'

'Yes.'

'And...?'

'I told Seraphina to go and take a babymoon.'

'What?'

'She called to congratulate us and ask for the wedding date and I suggested she book something right away and tell her husband how much she needed a break.'

'You said that?'

'Oh, yes.' Carmen nodded. 'I didn't want her here today. I wasn't having her ruining this for a second.'

They watched as Capricorn began labouring and pushing, until a tiny grey foal slipped out. What a privilege it was to watch Capricorn nudge her foal and see two shaky little front legs pushing up, the back legs unfolding into a stand…

'He's tiny!'

'Not for long,' Elias said. 'Dom's going to have his work cut out in a couple of years.'

He looked at his wife who was smiling and crying and totally happy to get messy on her wedding day.

'What do we call him?'

'Taurus,' Elias said. 'You had me at Taurus too.' Carmen smiled when she thought back to that day on the pier and understood he had fallen in love then too. 'I decided that before I even proposed.'

'What if I'd said no?'

'Then I'd have had a constant reminder of the one I let get away.' He looked at her. 'Carmen, I saw the pregnancy testing kit in the drawer last night.'

'I was going to wait till after the wedding…'

'And did you wait?' He gave her a look. 'Of course you didn't.'

'Of course I didn't,' Carmen agreed, and as he wrapped her in his arms and she breathed in his delicious scent she told him the wonderful news.

'We're going to need a babymoon of our own. But the honeymoon comes first!'

So much to do…

So many reasons to love.

* * * * *

#4161 BOUND BY HER BABY REVELATION
Hot Winter Escapes
by Cathy Williams

Kaya's late mentor was like a second mother to her. So Kaya's astounded to learn she won't inherit her home—her mentor's secret son will. Tycoon Leo plans to sell the property and return to his world. But soon their impalpable desire leaves them forever bound by the consequence...

#4162 AN HEIR MADE IN HAWAII
Hot Winter Escapes
by Emmy Grayson

Nicholas Lassard never planned to be a father. But when business negotiations with Anika Pierce lead to his penthouse, she's left with bombshell news. He vows to give his child the upbringing he never had, but before that, he must admit that their connection runs far deeper than their passion...

#4163 CLAIMED BY THE CROWN PRINCE
Hot Winter Escapes
by Abby Green

Fleeing an arranged marriage to a king is easy for Princess Laia—remaining hidden is harder! When his brother, Crown Prince Dax, tracks her down, he strands them on a private island. Laia's unprepared for their chemistry, and ten days alone in paradise makes it impossible to avoid temptation!

#4164 ONE FORBIDDEN NIGHT IN PARADISE
Hot Winter Escapes
by Louise Fuller

House-sitting an idyllic beachside villa gives Jemima Friday the solitude she craves after a gut-wrenching betrayal. So when she runs into charismatic stranger Chase, their instant heat is a complication she doesn't need! Until they share a night of unrivaled pleasure on his lavish yacht, and it changes *everything*...